You're
You

You're You

METTE BACH

JAMES LORIMER & COMPANY LTD., PUBLISHERS
TORONTO

James Lorimer & Company Ltd., Publishers acknowledges the support of the Ontario Arts Council (OAC), an agency of the Government of Ontario, which in 2015-16 funded 1,676 individual artists and 1,125 organizations in 209 communities across Ontario for a total of $50.5 million. We acknowledge the support of the Canada Council for the Arts, which last year invested $153 million to bring the arts to Canadians throughout the country. This project has been made possible in part by the Government of Canada and with the support of the Ontario Media Development Corporation.

Cover design: Shabnam Safari
Cover image: Shutterstock

Library and Archives Canada Cataloguing in Publication

Bach, Mette, 1976-, author
        You're you / Mette Bach.

"Real love."
Issued in print and electronic formats.
ISBN 978-1-4594-1258-3 (softcover).--ISBN 978-1-4594-1259-0 (EPUB)

        I. Title.

PS8603.A298Y68 2017   jC813'.6   C2017-903315-8
                                               C2017-903316-6

Published by: Distributed in Canada by: Distributed in the US by:
James Lorimer &   Formac Lorimer Books   Lerner Publisher Services
Company Ltd., Publishers   5502 Atlantic Street   1251 Washington Ave. N.
117 Peter Street, Suite 304 Halifax, NS, Canada   Minneapolis, MN, USA
Toronto, ON, Canada   B3H 1G4   55401
M5V 0M3   www.lernerbooks.com
www.lorimer.ca

Manufactured by Friesens Corporation in Altona, Manitoba, Canada in July 2017.
Job #234935

For Tony, who taught me that
we have to believe we are magic.

"Nothing is absolute. Everything changes, everything moves, everything revolves, everything flies and goes away."

Frida Kahlo

Freyja and Rachel

IT WAS THURSDAY AFTERNOON. Freyja and Rachel were in the closet shooting their weekly video blog, Out of the Closet. The video camera was strapped to the back of Freyja's desk chair and pointed at them. So when Rachel surprised Freyja with a kiss on the cheek and laughed, Freyja tensed up. She wasn't used to going off script.

"The list, the list," Rachel said, giggling. That's how they always ended.

"Yes. Let's get serious. Okay, today's list is called . . ." Freyja's eyes got big. Her brow furrowed. "What's the list today?"

Rachel, still giggling, shook her head at how easy it was to rattle Freyja. She said, "Reasons to Love Yourself, silly."

"Oh yeah," Freyja said. "Number one. No one else is like you."

"Number two." Rachel took over. "You outswam a lot of sperm to become the human being you are right now. You deserve to be here. So be here."

"Outswam sperm?" Freyja repeated. She made a face. "Gross."

"It's true. We all did." Rachel's certainty was one of the reasons Freyja fell in love with her. She could speak with authority on the weirdest stuff.

But outswimming sperm was not an image Freyja wanted in her head. She frowned. Time to interrupt. "Number three. You have a whole community of people. We love you and care about you and want to see you succeed."

"Okay, enough queer love for today," Rachel said to the camera. "And now . . . the moment you've all been waiting for. Two lesbians making out."

Rachel pulled Freyja to her and kissed her. Freyja was just about to lose herself in Rachel's warm mouth when she remembered the camera was on. She pulled back.

"You know," she said to Rachel. She pushed her blonde dreadlocks away from her face. "I really don't know about playing into some straight guy's fantasy of girls kissing."

Rachel looked at the camera and shook her head. "She overthinks everything." Then she looked at Freyja and said, "Stop thinking so much. Shut up and kiss me."

So Freyja did.

They both waved goodbye to the camera. After five seconds of waving and kissing, Freyja jumped up to turn the camera off. "I think we've got it. That's a wrap!"

Rachel followed Freyja into the bedroom. She put her arms around Freyja's waist and rested her cheek against the back of Freyja's neck.

"We should edit and upload," Freyja said. She

didn't want to get distracted. Getting the video post out was important.

"Really?" Rachel asked. "I was sort of hoping we could make out some more. Maybe do more than make out."

Rachel always started something after Out of the Closet. Knowing they had an audience got Rachel hot. She kissed the back of Freyja's neck, her trick for making Freyja forget everything. All Freyja wanted to do was give in to the desire. She wanted to throw Rachel on the bed and climb on top of her. Never mind that they had done it hundreds of times before. No matter how many times they had sex it was never enough.

Despite the tingle on her skin and the desire centred deep in her body, Freyja said, "We have to get this uploaded."

Rachel rolled her eyes. "You're no fun." She crossed her arms.

"Think of our viewers," Freyja said.

Rachel sighed. "I know, I know. But when do I get to think of us?"

01 Dumped

"THIS IS GOING TO BE HUGE," Freyja said to Rachel. They walked hand in hand toward the crowd that had already gathered for the Pride parade.

Freyja sounded confident, but her eyes darted around, hoping not to see certain familiar faces. Here in Abbotsford, Freyja had dealt with the worst bullies of her life. They had made life so awful she'd had constant stomach aches and nosebleeds. After moving with her dad to East Vancouver, Freyja had never looked back.

Then Freyja had met Rachel. After that, she realized she wanted to support other kids in finding love on their own terms, the way she had. That's why she and Rachel started Out of the Closet.

"Freyja!"

There was Cass. Together, Cass and Freyja had organized the first ever Pride parade in Abbotsford. Today it would snake through the heart of the Bible Belt town.

"Hey!" They ran to each other. It was strange for Freyja to see Cass in real life, not as a face on a screen. They'd come so far together. Cass still ran the GSA — Gay-Straight Alliance — that Freyja had started. Cass still had to face that horrible group of people every day.

Rachel stood off to the side while Freyja hugged Cass.

"Looks like a good turnout," Cass said. "Media's here."

Freyja saw that a couple of TV and radio stations had come to report on the event. She had hoped that the parade would be big enough, important enough.

But you couldn't predict things like that. It was the Fraser Valley, so the weather kept people in a lot of the time. Sometimes a big news story broke and took up all the media coverage.

But not today. Today was full of rainbows and triumph.

"I can't believe we pulled it off, Cass," Freyja said.

Cass smiled. "I know, right? The mayor's coming. You'll have to shake his hand after you go to the podium. Then say something inspiring. Something amazing."

Freyja had waited her whole life for this. From the time she was a kid, she'd watched heroes at podiums rousing the crowds. Martin Luther King, Jr., Harvey Milk, Gloria Steinem. Freyja had dressed as Nellie McClung for Halloween when she was twelve. She had read Simone de Beauvoir. She listened to Nina Simone and Buffy St. Marie. She was ready.

In the midst of the bustle, Freyja turned to Rachel. She noticed that Rachel looked sad. She was wearing her "This is what a lesbian looks like" T-shirt. She had rainbows painted on her cheeks. But she didn't look like someone who was about to lead a victory march through a conservative town.

Freyja tried to hug her. Rachel backed off.

"What's wrong?" Freyja asked.

"Ugh," said Rachel. "Everything." She looked Freyja in the eyes and said, "I can't do this anymore."

"What? The parade?"

"No," Rachel said. "Us. You. This."

It took Freyja a moment to realize what Rachel was saying. "Wait, you're breaking up with me?"

"You don't need me, Freyja. You've got hundreds of adoring fans. Even a bunch of journalists want a piece of you. Go be in the spotlight. Go be you."

Freyja couldn't believe what she was hearing. Today of all days! "Rachel, your timing is shit. Can you wait, like, fifteen minutes? I'll be off the stage and we can talk."

"I'm sick of being your sidekick. Your arm candy." She was in tears.

"You're none of those things. You're everything

to me. Come here." Freyja went for a hug again. But Rachel turned and bolted.

Freyja stood there, frozen. She wanted to run after Rachel. She called out, "Rachel! Don't leave me! Don't! No!"

For some reason, Freyja's feet wouldn't move. Maybe it was because she knew she was supposed to march — but the other direction from where Rachel had gone. She crouched over, feeling like she was going to vomit. Freyja was supposed to lead the flock, be an example. She watched Rachel disappear into the crowd. Two years of her life disappeared with her.

Freyja whipped out her phone. She texted, "Don't leave. I have to do this. But then we'll talk."

Send.

"You can't leave me. I don't know who I am without you."

Send.

"You're everything to me."

Send.

"I can't live without you."

Send.

"I'll come find you as soon as I'm done. It won't be long. We can fix this."

Send.

Freyja could not find anywhere to be alone. There were people everywhere. From the corner of her eye, she saw Cass pointing one of the media people in her direction. Freyja had no choice but to keep it together. Stuff the feelings down. Swallow them. No time to cry.

She looked down at her hands. She was shaking. The crowd would think it was nerves. Everyone gets nervous before they give a speech. She could hide that way, out in the open. No one would know the real reason she felt scared and alone.

"And now the moment we've all waited for," the MC said from the stage. "One of the youngest Pride parade organizers in history."

The crowd was made up of people of all ages. They laughed in a friendly way. *It's like they think I'm cute or something*, Freyja thought. Her dad and Gram waved at her. She couldn't see Rachel anywhere. She felt utterly alone.

But then Freyja thought of the kids in the crowd. They needed her to appear strong. She would do this for them even if she was falling apart inside. She knew what she had to do. She had to make sure students like her would feel safer in this community. They wouldn't have to move away like she did.

Breathe, Freyja told herself. She knew they expected good stuff, the stuff she'd practised in front of the mirror. They deserved it. She took the mic and looked out at the crowd.

"Hello out there," she began. There was feedback from the mic. It threw Freyja off. What was she supposed to say?

A technician came out and adjusted the mic. He passed it back to her and gave her an encouraging smile. That was all she needed.

She swallowed. She knew the words by heart.

"I couldn't be happier to be here today . . ."

When the parade was over, it was time for hugs. Gram, who didn't have much upper arm strength, gave Freyja the hardest hug ever. Her dad was so proud that he lifted her right off the ground.

"You were incredible up there," he said.

"Thanks."

"Where's Rachel?"

"She left me."

"What?"

"She dumped me. Right before I went up there."

"Oh, honey. I'm sure she didn't mean it," Gram said.

Her dad put his arm around her. He got it. He'd been left by a bunch of women.

"Should we look for her?" asked Gram.

"I think she must have taken the bus back," Freyja said.

Her dad patted her on the back. "Let's go home."

02 One Last Kiss

FREYJA SAT IN THE BACK SEAT and stared out the window. Reality had stopped being reality. She was looking out at a world that made no sense.

She and Rachel fit together seamlessly. They had been drawn to each other from the moment Rachel asked for help in Math. Freyja, the new girl, had said she was the last person who could help with algebra. They had moved to the back of the class and made fun of the teacher. Then Rachel had followed Freyja to her locker. It was as if it was the most natural thing in the world that they would have lunch together. They had every lunch together after that.

It didn't take long for Rachel to invite Freyja over after school. Those first sleepovers had been confusing, with Rachel talking about how totally hot Ryan Gosling was. She had told Freyja she was straight for him. Freyja didn't even know what that meant.

Later, tangled in the sheets, their bodies sweaty and spent, Freyja was nervous. She didn't know how the following Monday she'd be able to pretend they were nothing but friends. Rachel, who had never so much as kissed a girl before Freyja, had announced their relationship to everyone online before Freyja had even told her dad.

Things were tense a lot between them. But they were passionate. Making up was addictive. Freyja sometimes wondered if they fought just so they could go at each other with frantic need.

Now the breakup was on a loop in Freyja's mind. It played in slow motion, every word weird and distorted. But even as she watched the mental footage, she couldn't believe that Rachel really wanted it to end. It wasn't real. It couldn't be real.

Freyja held her phone in her hand. No new messages from Rachel.

In her room, Freyja stared at a poster on the wall. Frida Kahlo looked back at her. Freyja finally understood the expression that was on Frida's face. It was the look of a serious loss of faith. Of heartbreak. Loneliness. She stared at Frida Kahlo for a long, long time. Then she cried.

Freyja's social feed started to fill with messages. They were all "oh no" and "I'm sorry to hear it." Great. Rachel had already told people. Freyja read a couple of "do you want to talk about it?" texts from people she didn't know all that well, people who seemed to care. It was horrible, like her life was on display.

What were they going to do about the video blog? She and Rachel had hosted their show for over a year. It was growing. They had actual subscribers. Not many, but still. How was she supposed to tell their followers that they were no longer together? The account was in Freyja's name. She was the one who did it all — the filming, the editing, the uploading. Rachel didn't even respond to comments. Freyja was the one who had to deal with this. With everything.

Freyja opened the drawer in her desk. She got out a large pair of scissors. She looked at her wrists. They were covered in bracelets that Rachel had given her. Some were leather strips. Some were plastic cords. Some were beaded. One was torn fabric from the hem of Rachel's vintage skirt. They had become part of Freyja's personal style. They were a constant reminder of who she was, what she was. They showed Freyja and the world who loved her and whom she loved.

They had to go.

She put "Blow Me One Last Kiss" by Pink on repeat and searched the lyrics online. She read through one round of the song, sitting in her swivel chair with the scissors in her right hand. As round two of the song started, she turned up the volume and pulled her garbage can out from under the desk. Then, one by one, she snipped each bracelet off her left arm. As each band fell into the trash, it released a memory of Rachel tying it on her. It was odd to see the pale skin of her left wrist again. Freyja had almost forgotten what her arms looked like without the proof of the love between her and Rachel.

It took many repeats of the song before she was done. There was a big pile in the garbage to look at now. She stared at the mixture of empty Haagen Dazs tubs and Rachel's love tokens, candy wrappers and foil packaging. Then an even more depressing thought entered her mind. She had comforted herself with junk food: the sweetness of ice cream, the childhood taste of Pop Tarts. But not everyone had equal access to food. Just like not everyone had equal access to love. She was curious about what other people did. What about sad people who couldn't afford to gorge themselves to bury the pain?

She should find out. A Google search on poverty and food access turned into hours of reading. Freyja found it awful to think about people around the world — even right here in Vancouver — not having enough to eat. But at least it got her thinking about something other than her own sorrows. She saw that she had always been wrapped up in her own experience of the world. Yet there were other people out there who suffered more than she could imagine. She looked down at her wrappers and felt guilty for taking her right to snacks for granted.

What was really important was coming up with a plan. This was Freyja's final year of high school. Her grades weren't up to snuff — not really. Her study habits had involved Rachel for two years. They weren't promising.

Freyja could get tuition covered through her mom's connection to UBC. But she would have to make the cut. That'd be impossible. School subjects held no interest for her. None of it seemed to matter in the real world, where everyone had smartphones and could look up stuff. You didn't need facts. You needed to prove yourself.

There was one thing Freyja had not shied away from. It was getting up on a soapbox and speaking her mind. She did it when they wouldn't let her play boys' soccer in grade five. She did it again in grade eight when she noticed that the school needed a better recycling program. She just did it this past weekend with Pride.

Freyja thought about what it'd be like to see Rachel at GSA meetings. That is, if Rachel would still show up. Suddenly the queer scene felt too small. Their GSA was like a small town Freyja wanted to run away from. She needed a break from it. Forget the video blog. Forget the followers and their offers of pity.

She carried the plastic garbage can downstairs. She took one last look at her own privilege and tossed the mess out for good. What she had found out about food justice nagged at her. Eating was a basic human right. It pained her to think that in a world where so many had so much, there were people who couldn't get by. She should do something about it.

Love be damned. She went back to her room and filled out the local food bank's online volunteer form.

03 To the Rescue

FREYJA WATCHED GRAM PULL on a bright orange tunic to go with her blue yoga pants. She applied the purple eye shadow pencil that she kept near the hallway mirror. Then she added a bit of pink lipstick and a dab of neroli oil. *The woman has sass, that's for sure*, thought Freyja. Freyja actually preferred Gram as a parental figure to her mom. Her mom never wore bright colours or scents. And she wasn't around, anyway.

Gram walked Freyja down Commercial Drive. They commented on everyone from the pushy florist to the young punks hanging on the corner. As they passed an Italian café, a couple of older Italian men sitting out front gave Gram the up-down look. Freyja noticed that Gram noticed. Gram sort of smiled to herself.

Gram was forever single. She made it very clear that her biggest joy in life was taking care of her son and grandkid. So of course she walked Freyja to the very first session of the volunteer program at the food bank. Just as they turned onto Raymur Avenue, Gram took a step away from Freyja and eyed her.

"What's on your mind, Gram?" Freyja asked.

"I was just thinking how other girls your age go to movies and buy make-up."

"You think I should wear make-up?"

Gram shook her head. "I guess that'd throw off the whole dreadlocks, pierced septum thing you're going for."

Freyja swung her hair and took a pin-up model pose. "You mean you don't love it?"

"I like it more than that time you shaved your head."

"Hey," Freyja said. "I gotta be me."

Gram smiled. They walked in silence for a while.

"You know, Freyja," she finally said. "You don't have to solve all the world's problems."

"I wouldn't be able to live with myself if I didn't try."

Gram stopped in her tracks and looked at Freyja. "I remember that feeling."

They walked a bit more, and then Freyja said goodbye to Gram. She took a deep breath before rounding the bend of Raymur Avenue. This was it. The new cause.

As she approached the building, she saw an ancient-looking car pulled over. The trunk lid was up, and there was a woman standing behind it. She leaned against the car, looking exhausted, as she talked to a guy. The guy was holding a large banana box overflowing with food. Freyja thought he looked about her age.

The guy rested the box on the back bumper as he

opened the trunk with the keys the woman handed him. She had a baby strapped to her chest, a crying toddler in a carrier in the car, and a small child standing next to her.

Just then, the young child took off.

"Hunter!" the guy yelled. The banana box fell to the ground.

The woman let out a loud grunt, like this had happened many times before. She shrieked, "Get back here! Hunter!"

The boy laughed as he ran. He darted across the street without looking. He bolted into the park.

The guy took off after the boy.

Freyja ran after them, her instinct carrying her.

"Stop!" the guy ordered.

Nothing. The boy was in his own world.

Freyja swerved, thinking the boy might change direction. When he did, she managed to put her hand on his shoulder. Only then did he stop, still laughing.

"Stop!" she ordered. "I mean it."

But he got away from her.

The guy lunged at the kid. He caught him and swung him up off his feet.

"I'm fast," the boy said, proud.

"You sure are," Freyja answered.

"Let's get you back to your family," the guy said, putting the boy down.

"No!" yelled the boy.

"Take my hand," the guy ordered.

He looked at Freyja. Without any words, they both knew what needed to happen. Each of them grabbed the boy by one hand. He was forced to walk between them. He struggled to get free, but Freyja had done this with kids at the co-op. She refused to let go of his bony little hand.

The three of them walked back across the street together. By the time they got to the car, the woman was almost in tears. "Thanks for bringing him back. He does this all the time. I hate it. I can't run after him." She gestured to the little one strapped to her and the toddler in the carrier.

"No problem," the guy said.

Freyja was stunned by how cool he sounded, like he saved kids all the time. He didn't seem fazed at all. Freyja echoed his words, but her heart was racing.

Once again, the guy lifted the banana box to the trunk. She watched how composed he was. She had noticed that his dark brown eyes sparkled when the two of them had silently conspired to march the kid back. She felt there was something oddly familiar about this guy. There was something about him that made her feel like she'd known him all her life.

"I gotta go. I'm late," Freyja said.

"Thanks again," the woman responded.

The guy pointed his chin in Freyja's direction and said, "Thanks for helping."

"All good," she said. Suddenly, she felt like a dork. And she wasn't sure why. The guy smiled at her. Her mind flashed back to Rachel going on and on about Ryan Gosling. And that's when she figured out what was weird about all of it. Freyja thought this guy was attractive.

Freyja climbed the stairs to the entrance of the large building. Inside she was greeted by a woman at a desk.

"I'm here to volunteer," Freyja told her. "Sorting."

"Okay, they're almost ready to start."

Freyja pulled out her phone to check the time. She hated being late. "I'm sorry. Can I use the washroom first?"

"Of course. It's just up the stairs."

In the privacy of the stall, Freyja put herself into a power pose. Her hands on her hips, she mimicked Wonder Woman. She knew that body language had a huge impact on people. And these were all new people. She had to win them over. *That's the only thing to do when you're an outsider*, she thought. *You have to get people on your side and show you're not a victim.*

Freyja had thought her victim days were over. But Rachel breaking up with her brought those old feelings back. And she hated being taken by surprise. The chaos with the kid outside was a lot to handle. And a random hot guy? She was glad she'd never see him again.

She remembered Gram's advice to stop and breathe and regroup whenever she became nervous.

She wiped tiny beads of sweat from her forehead and checked herself in the mirror. She took a final breath and told herself it would be okay.

Freyja made her way down the rickety stairs into the warehouse. There was a group of people already gathered.

"Is this where the volunteers are meeting?" Freyja asked.

"Yeah, we're just waiting for the team leader. There he is now."

"Cool."

Freyja's jaw dropped. It was the guy from outside.

04 The Cause

"I'M SANJAY," SAID THE GUY. He was talking to everyone, but he looked right at Freyja. "Thank you for being here. This is important work. Most of us don't think about food until it's meal time. How many of you have eaten today? Yes, a donut and a coffee for breakfast counts."

Freyja raised her hand. She felt weird, being just one of the crowd with her hand up.

Sanjay continued. "Food and water are things that

we simply can't live without. The fact is that different people have different access to healthy food and clean water. It's one of the main social issues in the world today. And I'm not just talking about 'people starving in India.'" His fingers made air quotes and he smiled. "Just because that's where my family comes from. Look around. In this city, there are families who don't know where their next meal will come from."

Freyja found herself nodding. She knew how hard it was to get people's attention. But this guy had them all caring, at least for now, about food justice.

Sanjay made a gesture that included all of them. But again, he was looking at Freyja. "As volunteers you will be doing things that no one gets noticed for. But they are crucial to getting food resources out there. What happens in this warehouse is a lot of hard work. I hope that I can also make it fun for you guys. Can each one of you tell us a bit about yourself?"

He gestured to a little old lady, who said her name was Gladys. She said she had needed the food bank when she first arrived in Canada thirty years ago.

Now she was looking to give back. There was a carpenter who liked to travel and had settled here. One girl worked at Louis Vuitton serving rich people all day. She said this made a good balance. There was an office worker who was into health and nutrition. There were some giggly high school girls who confessed that they were there because they needed the volunteer hours.

Then it was Freyja's turn.

"I'm head of the GSA at my school," she said. "I'm hoping to put my skills in political activism to good use. You know, for the cause."

People nodded, but Freyja felt judged. She could almost hear them think, *Yeah, of course the girl with the dreadlocks and pierced face runs the GSA.* Sanjay looked blankly at her for a moment, and she suddenly felt silly for what she had said.

He quickly turned back to the group. "Okay," he said, clapping his hands together like a coach. "I'm going to split you into smaller groups. Let's start by sorting through the food donations that just came in."

He gestured to the massive bins behind him. They were filled with bags of stuff from pantries and things people had tossed into donation boxes.

Freyja was surprised. Maybe there was a whole world of nice people who gave stuff to the food bank.

"Always check the expiration date," Sanjay said. He picked up a can. "If it's expired, we can't give it to the public."

And maybe not.

"You mean it's garbage?" Gladys asked.

Sanjay nodded. "Compost, but yeah. Same goes if the package has been opened or tampered with. And we can't give out homemade foods, like a mason jar of jam."

Freyja watched Sanjay. He was tall. He had warm brown eyes, clear skin, and a nice build — if you liked that sort of thing. He spoke with confidence. Freyja knew how hard it was to get a group of people onside. This guy knew what he was doing. He seemed to really believe in what he was saying.

Freyja wondered if he was popular in school. She wondered if he had a girlfriend. She hated that she thought that way — it seemed shallow. But if he was popular, she didn't know if she could deal with him. She had been burned too many times to think that insiders and outsiders could meet in the middle.

For Freyja, the GSA had been a raised middle finger to the popular guys and mean girls. Sure, anyone was welcome in the GSA. But if those fakey-fakes had tried to infiltrate, Freyja would have booted them out. Freyja was serious about creating safe spaces for outsiders like her.

As Freyja thought, she sorted quickly. She found she had a knack for finding best-before dates, no matter how well they were hidden. Sanjay had set them a challenge to find the worst food donation. And here it was — a pouch of ranch dressing. It was all faded and gross, and it was hard to make out the numbers on the packet. But it looked like it dated back to the 1990s.

Freyja left her station. She walked over to where Sanjay was talking with a delivery driver on top of a loading platform. She climbed the ladder. "I found this," she said as she held out the pouch.

"Score!" Sanjay yelled and put out his hand.

As Freyja passed the packet to him, their hands brushed lightly. Freyja noticed that Sanjay's skin was rough. And warm. There was something in that touch that made it hard to look at him. Maybe she just wasn't used to being close to straight guys.

"Listen up, everyone." Sanjay said. "I think we have a winner here, a display for the Wall of Shame." He held up the ranch dressing and squinted at it. "Freyja found this and it's from . . . let's see . . . 1998."

Everyone grimaced. "Eeewww," someone said.

Gladys said, "Some people in my building have things like that in their cupboards."

The office worker said, "They shouldn't. I think it qualifies as a biohazard."

"Food is food," Gladys said, shrugging.

Freyja was shocked. There were people who'd eat stuff that had been made and sold before she was even born? She wondered about their lives. Were they too poor to buy food, or maybe couldn't leave their apartments? Her mind boggled over it, and it made her sad.

Sanjay took control. "When you find things like this, bring them to me. I'll show you how we dispose of them. No one is going to get stuff like this from us."

Freyja was still standing next to Sanjay on the platform. She looked down at the volunteers going back to work. *This is a good vantage point*, she thought. *You can really see everything from up here.* But it was time to get back down on the ground.

Freyja sifted through the bins for the next couple of hours. She felt like a worker bee and she wasn't used to it. She was always the leader. Any group. Any sport. Any activity. Ever since bullies taught her what it was like to be on the bottom, she vowed never to be there again. She made sure she was the one who chose the team, the one who spoke for everyone. Here, sorting through canned goods and boxes of macaroni and cheese, she felt like one of the crowd.

Sanjay walked around, chatting and checking for questions. He asked Freyja's team what people liked to cook. Gladys said she liked to make borscht.

"And you, Freyja?" he asked.

"I don't cook."

"Never?"

"Never."

"So what do you eat?"

"Whatever's around. Pizza Pops. Hot dogs. This stuff." She held up a box of mac and cheese.

"What about veggies?" Sanjay asked.

"Ketchup's a veggie, right?"

Sanjay's eyes widened. It looked like he was trying to form words. But they would not come. He turned and walked away.

It was close to six o'clock by the time Sanjay came back. Freyja was finishing up.

"Is your boyfriend picking you up?" he asked.

Freyja laughed. It wasn't a kind laugh. So that was Sanjay's real reason for being here. It was a good place to meet girls. Not girls like Freyja. But maybe those girls who flipped their hair a lot.

"Um . . . dude, I'm queer."

"Oh. Sorry." He frowned. "Not sorry that you're

queer. I mean, sorry that I assumed. I didn't mean anything by it."

"People like you never mean anything by it."

"People like me? What's that supposed to mean? Brown guys?"

"No!" Freyja was deeply insulted. She would never say something racist like that. "No, you know. Popular guys."

"Who are you calling popular?"

Freyja looked at the floor. Why did she even bother talking?

"So, uh, see you again next week?" Sanjay asked.

She looked him in the eye. "I'll be here."

"Uh, great." He sounded polite, like someone working a customer service desk. "See you then, then." He smiled, but it seemed forced.

As Freyja walked away, she worried she'd just made things awkward between them. It occurred to her that he was just trying to be nice.

05 Back in Charge

THE NEXT AFTERNOON, Freyja walked into the GSA meeting with her head held high. It was bad enough that everyone knew Rachel dumped her. It was also obvious there was something going on between Rachel and Vanessa. Sure enough, Rachel was sitting with Vanessa.

Freyja would be in the spotlight for the first ten minutes or so of the meeting. And that meant she had to have swagger. She needed something big. Something distracting.

"So, like, there's homophobia everywhere," she started. Everyone had settled with their snacks or phones out in front of them. "Yesterday I volunteered at the food bank — it's my new thing. And someone there asked if my boyfriend was coming to get me."

One of the grade elevens laughed.

"You?" Vanessa asked.

"I know, right?" Freyja said. She had to beat everyone to the punch line. "I mean, what about me says *boy*friend?" She looked down. "The ripped military pants? My Vans?"

The group laughed again. It got Freyja going. She loved being able to entertain, even if it was at her own expense.

"Maybe it's the dreads. Or this." She jiggled the ring in her nose. She glanced at Rachel. Rachel looked down. So eye contact was out.

"People make assumptions. That's homophobia," Freyja finished.

"Maybe they were just making conversation," Rachel offered. Her tone was cool, too cool. She wasn't being taken in by Freyja's display. And the worst part was that Freyja knew Rachel was right. Sanjay had just said it to be friendly. How could Rachel pick up on that?

Freyja quickly introduced the theme of the day. She had found a documentary about the AIDS crisis in the 1980s. She had been shocked to learn the death toll wasn't taken seriously because its effects seemed limited to gay people. In the dark ages of the 1980s, no one cared about gay people. So Freyja wanted to talk about how homophobia was still everywhere you went. Nowhere was really safe.

Deep down, Freyja knew that she overprepared because she was afraid to be around Rachel. She didn't know what to talk about except LGBTQ issues. And as bad as it was to talk in front of Rachel, it was worse when Rachel wasn't around.

All anyone asked Freyja about was how she was dealing with the breakup. "Horrible" was the honest answer. But no one wanted to hear that. Maybe they did, but Freyja didn't want to talk about it.

The doc was already screening when John showed up. He was late and loud as usual, throwing open the door to the darkened classroom.

"Sorry I'm late," he said.

Freyja wanted to shush him, but instead shot him a look and pointed to a chair at the back of the class. He ignored her and slowly made his way up to the front. He walked like a mime, every step too big, too precise. It made him even more distracting.

He finally took his seat. Then he slowly unzipped his bag, reached into it and brought out a bag of chips. He opened the crinkly bag and began munching. *Chew. Chew. Chew.*

"Pssst. John!" Freyja whispered. She shook her head and held her finger to her lips, librarian style. She mouthed the words *knock it off*. He was going for leadership of the GSA next year. Freyja doubted his ability to mentor others when his own behaviour was so bad.

John folded up the bag of chips, still being loud. He put it back into his bag.

Phew. Finally they could all focus.

Just then, John's phone vibrated. Instead of ignoring it, he took it out and texted.

At this rate, Freyja would never be able to step down as leader.

When the doc was done, they all had a chance to debrief their feelings.

Freyja had a final duty after the screening was over. "Okay, so, as a group, we need to decide where we're going to put our efforts. We've been asked to do a musical presentation for Diversity Day. But I think the invite was a bit of a stereotype. I mean, what are we? The cast of *Glee*?"

She got a few laughs for that. It spurred her to continue. "Transgender Day of Remembrance is coming up. I'm thinking it'd be great to make placards and organize a good old-fashioned walkout. We'll leave classes to protest the fact that we still don't have all-gender washrooms at this school."

She looked around. Everyone looked exhausted. *Jeez*, she thought. It wasn't like she'd told them they had to take part in the construction of the new washrooms themselves!

"Principal Anderson said the school got grandfathered on the washroom thing. It wouldn't be an issue if the school was newer," Vanessa explained.

"And that's good enough for you?" Freyja asked, raising an eyebrow.

"Well . . ."

"Well, you're not trans. I guess it doesn't matter to you, since it doesn't directly affect your life."

"Uh . . . I just think that it's a losing battle. We already know what the principal will say since he's already said it."

"That's what protests are for. To change what people think and say."

"Is there anyone at this school right now who even needs that washroom?" Vanessa asked.

"That's not the point," Freyja said. "This is about safe space. This is about human rights."

"I think we should do the musical number," John cut in. "I hear the drama club is putting on a short.

The band is playing. I dunno. I think it makes sense that they'd ask us to do something kind of, you know, *gay*." He paused. "I mean *gay* as in fun."

"Yeah!" Vanessa said. "We could totally do Beyoncé."

Freyja couldn't believe it. "Seriously?" She scanned the room. Her eyes settled on Rachel, who still wouldn't meet her gaze. "You guys would rather lip-sync than stage a protest?"

"Lip-sync?" John said. "Who said anything about lip-syncing? We're singing, baby." He did a little dance in his chair like he was fabulous.

Everyone laughed.

John called out, "All those in favour of Beyoncé?"

Hands started to go up all over the place. Vanessa was in right away, and she nudged Rachel. Rachel started to raise her hand, her eyes still fixed on the table in front of her. But then she glanced at Freyja and put her hand back down.

As hands went up, Freyja knew she didn't have the majority. She didn't seem to have anyone at all. But, she reminded herself, not everyone was present.

"Let's hold off on voting until next week," she quickly said. "Go off and think about it. Do some soul searching about your values. Then we can decide."

John got the attention of the group of girls across from him and rolled his eyes. They laughed. Freyja saw it, but she was used to that sort of thing. She had to be patient. They would all realize in time that the right thing to do would be to protest. She'd shown them the documentary. She'd explained to them that the rights they had now came as a direct result of the queer protests of the past. They had to see that they had no option but to keep fighting for what was right.

06 Different Directions

FREYJA COULD SEE RACHEL going to bolt for the door. She stood in the way. "Rachel, can we talk?"

Vanessa shot Rachel a look and said, "Meet me by my locker in ten minutes."

Rachel nodded at Vanessa and stood beside her seat. She fidgeted with the zipper on her bag. Freyja could almost see the wall between them. They used to tell each other everything. Freyja was able to read every single one of Rachel's facial expressions.

She could tell what was up by the tone of her voice. But now Rachel was guarded.

"What happened between us?" Freyja asked.

Rachel shrugged. "I think we're just going in different directions."

"I'll say. You wouldn't have chosen singing over human rights a few months ago."

"That's unfair. I have always loved singing. You know that."

"But seriously," Freyja tried to get their closeness back into her voice. "What was with John today?"

She and Rachel used to dissect John's behaviour after every GSA meeting. They could do it for hours.

"Today?" Rachel shrugged it off. "I didn't notice anything."

Freyja took the words like a punch to the stomach. "Who's being unfair now?"

"What? He has just as much a right as anyone to weigh in on plans. We're graduating this year. He'll be heading the GSA next year, whether you like it or not."

Freyja looked at Rachel and saw a stranger. She used to be able to hold her, touch her, kiss her. And now she stood across from her and saw someone she barely knew.

They'd always had different ways of seeing the world, and when they didn't understand each other, they usually wound up naked. Distracted. She studied Rachel's face, the lips that Freyja still felt drawn to no matter how she tried to ignore them. But now she could no longer have them.

"How did we get here?" Freyja asked.

Rachel shook her head. "I can't have this conversation. Not now."

She left.

As Freyja got to the food bank, she saw Sanjay out front again, helping a family load up some boxes.

She was very close before he noticed her. He took a step back and smiled.

YOU'RE YOU

"You came back. Solid," he said. "I like that."
He touched her arm. It was so gentle that she could barely feel it through her jacket and sweater. And, to her surprise, she liked it.

She smiled back. That was a good word to get called. *Solid.*

Freyja threw one of the big communal shirts over her outfit. She didn't want to get dirty like the last time. Even with an apron, it had been hard to avoid getting filthy. And that was just sorting packaged food. This time her team would sorting other stuff.

"Okay, folks," Sanjay announced. "Today we're doing apples. Anyone deathly afraid of spiders? You might see a few." He laughed nervously. "You probably won't. But you might."

"North Americans aren't afraid of dictators. But they're afraid of spiders," Gladys said.

Freyja saw a basket of granola bars put out for volunteers. She looked through before choosing a chocolate-dipped one with peanuts. She chomped down a bite of the chewy bar while listening to Sanjay explain what they had to do. She admired the way he took charge.

The work was pretty much disgusting. She put on blue latex gloves and went through boxes of apples, pulling out the rotten ones.

"Freyja," Sanjay said, walking over to her. "How goes?"

"Meh," she said. She gestured at the sea of apples in front of her. Her forehead was sweaty from all the bending and sorting. And with him standing there, it got worse.

"How's life?" he asked.

She shrugged. "Fine, I guess. I'm trying to get our GSA to stage a protest," she said without thinking. Then she was surprised she told him. "It's not working."

"Oh yeah, I saw you in the news."

"You did?" She blushed. The sweating was so embarrassing.

"I . . . we like to keep on top of our volunteers, what they're doing online, and so on."

"So you Googled me?" She was shocked, even though she Googled people all the time.

"Not just you," he said. She could see he was trying not to be weird. "I like to know what people are up to when they're not here."

"Oh . . ."

"My point is, you've done some impressive stuff. Your YouTube channel and all that."

"Oh, God. Tell me you didn't watch my videos."

"Just a couple."

"They're for LGBTQ youth," she explained. "It's not like I'm some popular online star or anything. I'm just trying to make sure that queer teens have information and support."

"It's cool you put yourself out there like that. Most people wouldn't."

"I do what needs to get done. Especially when no one else will."

He nodded. "I relate to that."

"You do?"

"I think people like getting credit. They like

taking a bow after the show is over. Most people don't like doing the actual work."

"But you do?" Freyja asked archly. "You like working?"

He nodded. "Each summer for the past few years I've gone to work on my mom's family's farm in India. And my uncle always gives me the toughest jobs that nobody wants."

"Wow." Freyja had not been expecting that. She tried to imagine him working in a field in India. But she couldn't.

"It's back-breaking stuff," he said. He lifted the box of sorted apples to the cart. "But I love it. It keeps me in check."

"What do you mean?"

"Growing up here, it's easy to take stuff for granted. Over there, it's still a big deal to feed your family, to get by."

"Huh." Freyja didn't know what else to say.

"I'm moving there for a while after school is over," he told her.

"To India?"

"Yeah. My uncle said if I do, he'll teach me ancient Indian farming practices. And then, if the stars line up, I want to bring those techniques and technology back to Canada. I've met organic farmers here already through the food bank, so . . ."

"You really have a plan." Freyja couldn't help but be impressed.

"What I have is a dream. The *plan*, according to my parents, is pre-med at UBC."

"Oh. So they don't know that you're going to be a farmer instead of a doctor?"

"I haven't told them yet."

"It's coming up kinda soon, isn't it?"

"Well, what's your plan?"

Freyja shrugged. "Definitely not pre-med at UBC."

"Oh?"

"My grades are lousy and my family has no money. I'll probably just work for a while. I'm thinking about moving to Ottawa."

"Ottawa? What for?"

"Politics, of course."

"Sounds like a pretty clear-cut plan."

He smiled. Freyja noticed his smile was kind of goofy. It seemed as if he wanted to say more. He opened his mouth to speak, but nothing came out. He nodded and moved on. His job was to talk to volunteers, so Freyja found it odd that he was tongue-tied.

When Freyja's cart was full of sorted boxes, she wheeled it to the loading zone. She stood by the posse of girls and waited for Dan, an older guy who was supposed to take the cart. The girls grumbled.

"Ugh. This is the worst. I'm totally ruining my manicure."

"We should suck up to that team leader guy. Maybe we can get better jobs."

"You're right. Let's invite him to our party."

"He's a kind of a nerd," one protested.

"There's something kind of intense about him," another said.

"He's way too serious."

"Whatever. If it'll get us out of this BS, it's worth a try."

Freyja couldn't listen any longer. She left the cart for Dan and went back to her station to sift through another box.

The rest of the shift, Sanjay stayed on the other side of the warehouse. He joked around with all the volunteers except for Freyja. The girls laughed loudly around him. Whenever she checked to see where he was, she caught him looking at her. But then he would quickly look away. It was like he went back and forth between liking her and snubbing her. *That's a bummer*, thought Freyja. Because, as much as she didn't want to, she quite liked Sanjay.

07 Making Conversation

FREYJA'S DAD TOOK A BIG TRAY of taquitos out of the oven. Dad, Gram, and Freyja each grabbed a plate, four of the crunchy rolls, a dollop of sour cream and a handful of tortilla chips. They headed into the living room to binge-watch *Sherlock*.

If there was one thing the three generations could agree on, it was that Moriarty was the perfect villain. Freyja also argued that Benedict Cumberbatch was not as good looking as the media made him out to be. The best part of this show, for her, was that when Sherlock really needed to think, he went into his mind palace. That was something she understood.

She wasn't Sherlock Holmes, but she too was often in her own world. She saw things in a way that others didn't and she couldn't understand why.

Her phone vibrated. She pulled it out from the pocket of her hoodie. There was a text from a number she didn't recognize.

"Sanjay here. You left without signing out. So I did it for you."

"Cool. Thanks." *Send.*

Her phone vibrated again. Odd.

"Next week I can take you out on deliveries. If you want."

"Okay." She texted back.

There was a third buzz a second later. "Let me know if there's anything else I can do to help."

"All right." *Send.*

When the phone buzzed again, her dad said,

"Wow. Someone more important than *Sherlock*? It must be love."

Gram laughed. Everyone knew that you didn't text and *Sherlock*.

"Just some guy from the food bank," Freyja said.

"A guy?" Gram asked. She raised her right eyebrow.

"The team leader," Freyja said defensively. "It's about my shift next week."

Dad and Gram both nodded. But they looked at each other and then back at Freyja. It looked like they didn't believe her.

"It sounds serious," Dad said.

"He sounds cute," Gram teased.

"What?!" Freyja rolled her eyes. "I'm a lesbian, remember?"

"Rewind a bit," Gram said to Freyja's dad. "You can't miss anything or you're screwed."

Just as Freyja's dad found the exact spot where their viewing got derailed, Freyja asked, "Is it weird that he just texted me three times in a row for no real reason?"

Her dad shrugged. "Do you like him?"

"No. I dunno." She made a face. "No. Not like that."

"Then don't worry about it."

"What do you mean?"

"Maybe he has a little crush on you."

"*A crush*?" she repeated. "Ewww!"

"News flash, daughter. Guys get crushes. If you don't feel anything back, don't worry about it."

"And be nice," Gram added.

"What? I'm not nice?" Freyja said in a huff.

"Let's just say, I'd hate to be *that* guy," Gram said, pointing at Freyja's phone.

"Can we just watch the show?" Freyja asked.

"God, I hope so," her dad said. He pushed play. Benedict Cumberbatch and Martin Freeman were back.

Freyja took a deep breath. She was walking along Raymur Avenue. It was drizzling and the sky was grey. It was a typical fall day in Vancouver, and with it came a reminder of the long winter ahead. Freyja liked the rain, though. She felt sheltered by the blanket of clouds that covered the city for a lot of the year.

She signed in and went out back to the warehouse. Sanjay was across the room. He looked at her and didn't smile or say hi. Freyja found it humbling. Why had she thought those texts meant anything? No way was her dad right with his crush theory.

Actually, it was a relief. The last thing she needed was that sort of complication. It had been years since any guy had approached her. But back when they did, it was always awkward and awful. Her dating life had been the worst until Rachel came along. Then everything was amazing. But now that Rachel was gone, it was all awful again.

Sanjay was talking with the girls when she approached. She could tell it wasn't about the work.

"Hey, uh, can I interrupt?" Freyja asked over the girls' chatter.

"Sure," Sanjay answered.

"I don't know what you want me to do this shift."

"Right," he said, looking around. "How about . . . follow me."

As she followed him toward the loading dock, Sanjay said, "I had this idea. Maybe we could go to the grocery store together. There's a manager I need to follow up with."

"Sure," said Freyja.

"She's cool. She wants us to pick up some stuff."

"Yeah. Cool." Freyja nodded. She liked the idea of not being in the warehouse.

"Okay," Sanjay said. "Wait here."

He went into the small office and spoke with Dan. Dan waved out the office door at Freyja. She waved back. When Sanjay came back out he was holding car keys. "Come on," he said.

They walked out into the rain.

"Do you need your jacket?" Sanjay asked.

"Nah. I'm okay."

"Cool."

Sanjay led Freyja to a rusty old pickup truck. Freyja could tell that it had once been red, but now it was orange after years of decay. Sanjay opened the passenger side door to let Freyja in.

"They let you drive this thing around?" she asked.

"It's Dan's," Sanjay explained. "He calls this thing the Beast."

Freyja laughed.

Sanjay said, "If you're afraid of riding in the Beast, we could take my grandmother's Toyota."

"Seriously?"

"Yeah. She works upstairs doing admin stuff."

"No way."

"That's how I got involved. Random fact about me? I've been volunteering here since I was six."

"Awwww," Freyja couldn't help but say. Sanjay at six must have been cute. "Your grandmother, eh? That's super cool."

Sanjay adjusted the rear-view mirror and buckled up. A big cloud of exhaust spread behind them as they turned out onto Venables. Pretty soon, they were headed along Hastings Street toward Burnaby.

"So, um," said Sanjay. "It's cool how you and Rachel are so open about your relationship in your video blogs."

"Okay. I'm finding it kind of creepy that you watched that. Anyway, Rachel dumped me."

"She did?" Their eyes met. He held her gaze a little too long for someone who should have been focused on driving.

She pointed straight ahead. "Watch the road."

"Shit. Sorry." He jolted into a stiff posture and turned his eyes forward.

"Yeah. Seven and a half weeks ago. That's why there haven't been any new videos. Kinda bites, actually."

"I bet."

"Yep. A kid in Australia messaged me wanting to know where Rachel is and when she'll be back. Another kid in Tennessee said she misses her."

"So what are you going to do?"

Freyja shrugged. "Advise them never to declare their love on the Internet?"

Sanjay chuckled. "Is that how you feel?"

"No," she admitted. "I just don't want to publicly break up."

"But your relationship was public."

"Yeah, but that was when it was good. Breakups suck."

"Yeah. That's true."

"So you've had your heart broken?"

"Uh . . . not exactly."

"No?" Freyja thought he seemed like the sort to have had at least one girlfriend. "Then why'd you agree with me?"

"I don't know. Something to say."

She grimaced.

"Well . . . breakups do suck," Sanjay said defensively. "I mean, I'm sure they do. Why wouldn't they? No one wants to break up."

"Rachel did."

"Well, she's an idiot."

"Why?"

"She broke up with you."

"You don't have to put her down."

"Sorry. I didn't mean to. It was just another one of those things to say."

"You say some super-weird things."

He sighed. "I'm just trying to make conversation."

"Sorry," Freyja said, remembering her Gram's warning about being nice. She thought it was funny that Sanjay wasn't as confident with her as he was with other people. Maybe it was what they were talking about. Maybe it was that she didn't mind him asking, because he was asking about her, not Rachel.

08 True Confessions

THEY PULLED INTO THE PARKING LOT of a small grocery store. Freyja liked that it wasn't one of the big chains. Sanjay walked up to the clerk like he knew her and asked for the manager.

"Wait right there," she said, reaching for her phone to send and receive a text. Then she told them, "She's coming in five minutes."

"Okay," Sanjay said.

Freyja and Sanjay stood silently side by side.

Then Sanjay leaned in and, in a very quiet voice, asked, "Do you want to play a game?"

"Always."

"Let's profile these customers by their groceries."

"Uh . . ."

"Like, what kind of people they are. For example," Sanjay dropped his voice to a whisper. "Here we have a single man. You can tell by the one piece of chicken and the asparagus."

Freyja eyed the guy in the sports jacket. He did look single. "Probably gay too," she added.

"Thought it. Wasn't going to say it," Sanjay said. The corners of his mouth tilted up in a smile.

"And here we have a typical frat guy," Sanjay said as the next guy got to the checkout. "A jock. Maybe a body builder. Cans of chilli, cans of tuna. Eggs. This guy's a protein fiend."

Freyja laughed.

She called the next one. "Mother. Popsicles. Ice cream in a bucket. Two packages each of hot dogs and hot dog buns? She probably has five kids or more."

"Another random fact about me? I've never had a hot dog."

"You've *never* eaten a hot dog?" Freyja could not believe her ears.

He shrugged. "Vegetarian. I grew up that way."

"Still. How'd you handle hot dog day at school?"

"Tofu dog."

Just then Sanjay took a step back and looked down. Then shifted his weight forward and leaned in toward Freyja again. "All right, fine. I'll tell you my deep, dark secret. But you have to promise not to judge me."

Freyja couldn't help but smile.

His voice got low and intense. "Sometimes . . . not often . . . but every now and then . . . I go through the drive-thru. And I get the worst thing anyone brought up in a woke Hindu household can eat."

"What's that?"

"A bacon burger," he said, looking guilty. "And I feel so ashamed. It's not just the beef and the pork. It's like everything I spend my life fighting in one super gross mess. We're talking hormone-injected cows and pigs that probably never saw daylight. There's corporate greed, first-world privilege. There are fossil fuels it takes to process everything and deliver the suffering right to your gas-guzzling car. Everything is wrong with it."

Freyja laughed. "It's not that bad, is it? My dad and I go for fast food once a week."

"Well, what's your thing then? Everyone has something."

"Oh," Freyja paused. She didn't like the idea of telling him. No one but Rachel knew this about her. "When I get really stressed . . . like only really, really stressed, I smoke."

"That's so bad for you."

"You asked."

After the manager and Sanjay talked, Freyja and Sanjay lifted milk crates of non-perishables onto a dolly, then they wheeled them to the truck.

On the drive back, Freyja remembered what Sanjay said about his grandmother. She thought about Gram. "Gladys is quite a character," she said.

"She totally is," said Sanjay. "She's a real survivor. I admire her."

"Yeah."

"You know, she lived off the land for a while. Then came to Canada as a refugee."

"Wow."

"Yeah. I mean, I've got my stuff all ready to go in case of world disaster. But she's actually lived through it."

"You afraid of the zombie apocalypse, or what?"

"Nah. More like humanity. Water wars. That kind of thing."

Freyja gave him a puzzled look.

"You know the CEO of Nestle doesn't believe that access to water is a human right?"

"Well, yeah, but . . ."

"'Canada's got plenty of natural resources. We'll be fine,'" he spoke in a fake casual tone people use to reassure children. "But it's not true. Our rivers and resources have mostly been sold off. Truth is, we're effed."

"Paranoid much?"

"More like prepared."

"So that's why you want to learn traditional farming? So you can live off the land when the shit hits the fan."

"Yes." He said it with no irony at all.

It scared Freyja to think of someone her age having such a bleak outlook. Usually she was the one getting called "intense." But she had to admit that it was comforting that he took the fate of the world to heart.

"So how do you prepare for the end of the world?" she asked.

"Equipment. I've got a whole room full of stuff. Water filtration systems, a solid tent, knives, food supplies, hiking boots, compass, topographical maps. Books with information that most people rely on the Internet for. What if there's no Internet?"

Freyja laughed. "That'll be the day."

"Could happen."

"I guess."

"How would you meet up with your family if something happens? Do you have a plan if your phone suddenly stops working?"

"Uh . . . no . . . I'd go home, I guess."

"And what if they're out looking for you?"

"They'd go home sooner or later."

"What if there's a flood, or a power outage? Or somehow you can't access your home? Or it's unsafe?"

"I dunno. We'd probably find each other raiding the freezers at the Il Mercato market."

"So you'd be without a plan and you'd probably never see them again."

"Harsh, man."

"I'm just surprised. You seem all political and informed. But you're pretty confident that the world will keep going on like it does now."

"Well, I'm not paranoid."

"I'm not either."

"You're just ready for anything."

"Well, yeah. Like I said, *prepared*. With the world as it is, you have to be."

Freyja marvelled at how smart and even practical Sanjay was. He was the sort of guy who could start a fire in the wilderness with nothing, probably spear a hare if he had to. The kind of guy you wanted around in case of emergency.

The strangest part was that the whole time she was with Rachel, Freyja was always the serious one. She was the one who came off as paranoid about the state of the world and humanity. Rachel used to look at her the way she had just looked at Sanjay, with the suspicion that she was too negative for her own good. It was odd for Freyja to be the lighthearted one.

09 Being Prepared

WHEN THEY GOT BACK to the food bank, Sanjay got right to work. Freyja went back to sorting. The girls had all reapplied lip gloss and were standing around checking their phones. They'd all uploaded the exact same group shot of the four of them. Now they were competing to see whose photo could get more Facebook likes the fastest. Freyja kicked herself for eavesdropping on them. But she couldn't help it. They brought out her inner sociologist.

When Sanjay went to inspect their work, Freyja was mostly shielded from their view by a large skid of potatoes. She continued to sort silently. But she could hear them and paid close attention to what was going on.

The leader of the girl pack flipped her hair over her shoulder. "What are you doing this weekend?" she asked Sanjay.

Freyja wanted to disappear. She felt like she should, but didn't know where to go. If she were to step out now, it would for sure look like she was spying.

"Not much," he said.

"Well, I'm having a party, if you want to come."

"Oh," Sanjay said. "Maybe."

"Give me your phone. I'll give you my address."

He handed her his phone and she keyed in the numbers before passing it back. Freyja felt like the girl had taken a dagger, shoved it into Freyja's gut, and was twisting it around. Why did she feel that way? It's not like she had plans with Sanjay. It's not like she was interested in him.

Maybe she was hurting from Rachel. That was it. It was being broken-hearted. It was the loneliness of being an outsider. She would never willingly go to a party put on by girls like that. But she would also never get invited.

Sanjay thanked them for the invite as the girls left.

Freyja's hands were all mucked up from flattening dirty banana boxes. She stayed put when Dan joined Sanjay on the loading dock. Once again, Freyja thought she should make her presence known. But how?

"What was *that* about?" Dan asked. He was dad-like and seemed to know Sanjay well.

"Beats me. They wanted me to go to some kind of party."

"So are you going?"

"No way."

"I don't get you, man. You complain you never meet girls. But then a bunch of them want you to go to a party and you say no."

"They're not . . . I don't know. Not my type, I guess."

"What are you? Gay?" Dan asked. Freyja was put off by the idea that no straight guy would turn down the chance to be around those four. "I mean, it's cool if you are."

"No, I just . . . I don't know. Those girls stress me out."

"So let me guess. Instead of a party, you're going to go to the military surplus store."

"I was planning on picking up a new multi-tool. There's this one I've been eyeing that has a wood saw."

"Tell you one thing. You won't be meeting girls there."

"Maybe not," Sanjay said. Was that regret or relief in his voice?

"Man, you really don't see what's right in front of you."

"That's where you're wrong, man. I see things pretty clearly."

"You'd rather hang out with your lesbian friend, wouldn't you?"

Sanjay shrugged. "I wouldn't say no."

Freyja didn't know what to do. She wasn't meant to overhear that conversation. Some things were private. That was *super* private. She had to wait until they passed. She heard a jump. Then thesound of hiking boots crash landing on flat cardboard.

"Freyja?" Sanjay was standing behind her.

"Uh . . . hi." *Busted.*

"How long have you been there? I thought you left."

"I'm going now."

"Don't forget to sign out this time."

"I won't."

Freyja felt like she'd been caught, like she was sneaking around. But she hadn't been spying on him on purpose, had she? She couldn't get away fast enough.

Freyja had the contents of the kitchen cupboard spread out. The items covered the whole counter. There were granola bars and batteries and old bottles that needed to be recycled. It was a mess.

"What are you doing?" her dad asked as he walked in.

"Trying to get us prepared. You know, in case of an emergency."

"Like a *Sherlock* marathon emergency?"

"No. Earthquake, total collapse of the world economy . . ."

"There's all kinds of stuff in the storage room. We'll be fine."

"Get serious, Dad. If things go really wrong, people will totally freak out. They're not going to be nice to each other. All the tensions that are just below the surface are going to come bubbling up. There will be fist fights and people will threaten to kill each other over food and water."

"And you think having a few granola bars and some matches is going to help?"

"We don't have a plan about where to meet. What if our phones don't work? What if there's no more Internet?"

He shrugged. "We'll deal with it."

"I just want to make sure we have supplies to last at least a few days. Things like water and emergency food and candles for heat."

"You're a wise one, Freyja Jakobsen," her father said, like he was talking to Yoda. With that, he grabbed a couple of the granola bars and walked away.

"You know you just raided the emergency stash," Freyja called at his retreating back.

He stuck his tongue out at her and was gone.

10 Who You Are

FREYJA WAS IN HER ROOM, sitting on her bed. She leaned on a couple of lumpy pillows propped up against her headboard. She opened her laptop. Maybe she'd check in on some of the YouTubers she followed. Before she even got a chance, she noticed that Rachel had changed her Facebook status back to "in a relationship." There was a new, cute photo of Rachel and Vanessa together. And there was a message from Rachel in Freyja's inbox.

"I should have told you about Vanessa."

Freyja wanted to write back, "Get over yourself." She didn't like that Rachel thought that it meant that much to her. She didn't want Rachel thinking she had that much power over her. But she did. It was coming up on nine weeks since their last video blog. Freyja still couldn't bear to tell the world that she'd been dumped.

She wrote back: "You look happy. That's all that matters."

Rachel's typing bubble came up right away. Freyja waited.

There was a buzz.

"I thought you hated me."

Freyja typed back right away: "I could never hate you."

"Why have you been ignoring me then?"

"I'm ignoring everyone. It's not personal."

"Then you'll answer your phone."

Freyja's phone rang. Rachel's smiling face came up on the screen. Freyja made a mental note to change the picture. It was the adorable one taken last July at a picnic when they were both so in love. Now that smiling face made Freyja cringe.

"Hey," Freyja said.

"So you really don't hate me?" asked Rachel. "Even for getting together with Vanessa so soon?"

"I guess I suspected all along that you were into her."

"I never cheated, just so you know."

"It's fine, Rachel. It's really all fine. You deserve to be happy."

"Thank you."

"And I get that she's more fun than me."

"Freyja," Rachel said in a pleading way. Freyja could tell she didn't want to talk about it.

"It's okay, Rachel. I'll never be like Vanessa. I'm cool with it."

"So what are you keeping busy with lately? Seeing as you're ignoring everyone."

"Food bank mostly. Learning all kinds of stuff about food security. Food justice. That kind of thing."

"God, Freyja, you're so intense."

"I'm really not. I just . . . I don't know. I feel like the world could be better, you know?"

"Sometimes it's good to cut loose. Just have a good time."

"Like Vanessa." Freyja could tell she sounded jealous as soon as the name was out of her mouth. But it wasn't that she envied Vanessa or wanted to be like her. She really didn't. The whole "here for a good time, not a long time" attitude seemed lazy and selfish. But the world is full of people who are different. There are partiers. And then there are people whose idea of a fun time is guessing at other people's lives by the groceries they buy. That game with Sanjay was the most fun Freyja had had in ages.

"Vanessa's not that bad." Rachel's voice cut into Freyja's thoughts. "I think you'd like her if you got to know her."

Why would I want to do that? Freyja thought. But she said, "I'm just glad you're happy. That's the only thing that counts."

"You know what? I really miss you."

Freyja was surprised to hear Rachel say it. The phrase was a constant between the two of them. Rachel used to say it when they weren't together for just a few hours. Sometimes they'd spend every waking minute together because they couldn't bear to be apart. Freyja recalled when Rachel used to sleep over almost every night because they simply couldn't let go of each other. In some ways it seemed like yesterday. It felt like they should still have that.

Just then, another text popped up on Freyja's phone. It was Sanjay.

"You still up?"

Freyja texted back. "Yep."

"I should go," she said to Rachel. "It's late."

"Okay. See you soon?"

"Sure."

Sanjay had not sent anything after Freyja confirmed that she was awake. So she texted: "What are you still doing up? Chatting with a bunch of girls?"

"Well . . . you."

"Are the other ones all too busy for you?" She threw in a sad face emoji to tease him.

"No, cuz I saw you were online. I got to thinking about something you said."

"What'd I say?"

"You said you can't rely on people. You're always the one who has to step up. I thought I was the only one who felt that way."

"Nope. People suck."

"Ha! Yes."

"Face it. Our generation is useless."

"Totes."

Somehow, those few texts turned into a marathon that went on long into the night.

Sanjay asked Freyja about her favourite show. She told him it was *Sherlock*. He said *Elementary* was better. When she asked why, he explained that the Sherlock in that show cared about bee survival. That was the real way to save humanity. She told him she'd never seen *Elementary*. He told her she had to. She said she would.

She asked about his obsession with disaster. He told her he saw it more as self-reliance. He wanted to be able to handle things when they went wrong. That was why he had learned to tie knots and build shelters. That was why he wanted to learn farming skills instead of studying abstract sciences. He told her his parents didn't understand him because they were both academics. But his grandmother got it. She had spent her entire life growing vegetables and cooking them. All she wanted was to pass on that knowledge. But in his whole huge family he was the only one who cared about learning from her.

Freyja told him that she got the parental academic thing. She told him that her Gram didn't cook, but she had taught Freyja everything she knew about the world.

They talked about movies. Then music. They traded one song for another. They each sat alone in their bedrooms dreaming of the other one.

Freyja couldn't picture what Sanjay's room looked like. She wanted to ask him to send her a photo or take a video, but she didn't want to sound creepy or too curious. She told herself that if she was meant to find out, she would. It was weird, though, because he knew what her room looked like. He'd seen it on her video blogs. It had never bothered her that anyone on the Internet could see her room. But it made her feel self-conscious that Sanjay knew that she had a turquoise bedspread with orange trim and orange accent pillows. He knew she had a poster of Frida Kahlo. He knew she had an old-fashioned alarm clock. He had seen the picture of her and Dad on her nightstand. Freyja wanted to know these things about Sanjay. But instead she asked, "If you're so cynical about humanity, how come you dedicate yourself to the food bank?"

"Because food security is the only way to move forward. It's our only shot at survival."

She was about to type that he was too dramatic. But then he added something else: "Besides, every cynic I know is an idealist deep down inside."

It was 3:30 in the morning when they agreed to stop sending messages back and forth.

It took Freyja a while before she could roll over and fall asleep. She was drifting off to sleep when a panicked thought struck. What if this was just Sanjay's way? Maybe he stayed up texting with all kinds of people. As she turned that idea around in her mind, she realized that it mattered to her. She knew she had better just forget it. She should keep her cool and not get sucked into thinking too much about Sanjay. But thinking about him made her smile. Thinking about him made her feel understood. She had never realized what a rare thing that was.

11 Fighting the Power

FREYJA SAT IN FRENCH CLASS. She was trying to keep her eyes open, despite the awful pain of conjugation. She took another sip from the takeout coffee on her desk. Her stomach was acidic from drinking too much coffee. She had a case of the jitters. Her phone buzzed in her pocket.

Madame Hébert was writing on the electronic whiteboard, so Freyja snuck a peek at her phone. It was Sanjay. Freyja got a rush all over at the thought of him. It was almost as if her heart stopped for a beat.

A quick click revealed a picture of a yawning puppy. Underneath it, Sanjay wrote: "Me today. Totally worth it."

She quickly texted back: "LOL. I'm buzzing on coffee. Totally worth it."

Suddenly, Madame's hand came down hard on Freyja's desk. Freyja jolted back in her seat. The stern face of an elderly Acadian woman glared at her from less than a hand span away. Freyja gulped like a scared cartoon mouse about to get chased by a mean cat.

"What is the policy on cell phones in my class, please?" Madame Hébert asked.

"No cell phones."

"And what is that?" Madame pointed to Freyja's hands.

"A phone."

Madame put her hand out. Freyja meekly laid the phone in her hand. Madame took it and read the screen. *Oh God*, Freyja thought. *Oh God. She wouldn't. She couldn't.*

She did. "And who is this Sanjay?"

Freyja was totally stunned. "Uh . . . a friend?"

"Is this friend worth sacrificing your French mark?"

"Uh . . . no?"

Even as she was sitting there cowering and afraid, Freyja thought Madame's shaming of her publicly was uncalled for. It was bullying. But Freyja didn't know what to do about it. If you saw bullying you were supposed to report it to a teacher. What if a teacher was the one who made you feel like crawling under your desk out of fear?

Freyja couldn't concentrate for the rest of the class. She was too anxious. Her mind raced repeating her exchange with Madame Hébert. She wondered how else she could have answered. The right answer, of course, was that she shouldn't have been texting in class at all. But how could she help herself? There were forty-two more boring minutes left in the nightmare that was Français Langue 12.

Besides, it was Sanjay. Anyone else she could have resisted.

When class was over, Freyja put her books in the canvas book bag she carried around all day. She was just closing it over the bulge of her French book when John came over. He was wearing a purple T-shirt with a teal cardigan. Freyja noticed he had a touch of make-up on. His skin shimmered ever so slightly under the fluorescent lights.

"Who's Sanjay?" John asked.

"Oh, he's just this guy from the food bank."

"Just this guy?" John repeated. He sounded like he didn't believe her.

"Yeah," she said. "Why?"

"Oh, nothing. It was just the way you smiled when you got the text. I was daydreaming anyway, so that's how come I noticed."

"How did I smile?"

"Like someone who's hiding something."

"Dude. Look who you're talking to. You and I are the gayest gays in the GSA."

John shrugged. "It's a rainbow."

"I don't have some kind of secret boyfriend," said Freyja defensively. "Just so you know."

"Okay . . . okay."

John turned on his heel and left the classroom.

At the food bank, Freyja told the group about a documentary she had watched with her dad and Gram. They had hated it.

"It's about the unethical treatment of animals. How it's totally the same as the unfair way humans treat each other."

"I've seen that one," one of the girls said. "What's it called again?"

"Did you know we could have ended world hunger long ago?" asked Freyja.

Sanjay nodded. The girls stared with blank expressions as Freyja explained the way the food chain works, big manufacturing, migrant labour, and profit-hungry corporations. As the words poured from her, she felt that she was meant to say them. This was her true calling. She could see herself already. Next year, she'd get an old VW van and camp out in Ottawa. She'd make some noise. It was time for people to wake up and stop being so greedy. So she needed to become the perfect food activist role model.

"I'm becoming a vegetarian," she declared. "As of this morning. Actually, it started last night after the doc. But that doesn't count because I'd already had dinner."

"What'd you have?"

"Chicken strips."

"You didn't," one of the girls said. They laughed.

"Did you hear the chickens scream from somewhere deep inside you?" Sanjay asked with a smile. He rubbed his belly for effect.

She glared at him. "Are you making fun of me?" She knew the girls were, but she thought Sanjay would approve.

"No. No." He shook his head a little too hard for

someone who wasn't making fun. "It's just that . . . Don't take this the wrong way. But you're not the first person to see a doc, make a claim like you just did, and then two weeks later . . . hamburger time."

Freyja blushed at his reminder that she knew his deep, dark secret. "Yeah, well, you don't know how determined I am."

Freyja tried to hide it, but she was upset that Sanjay didn't take her seriously. There was no point in digging in her heels. She'd have to prove her resolve. And prove it she would.

"So how was the party?" Sanjay asked the girls. It was clear he was trying to change the subject.

"Great. It was lame you didn't come."

"I was busy," Sanjay said. "Like now. I should go do stuff." He waved his hand vaguely and then walked away.

The girls went back to the task at hand. Freyja was keenly aware that the only time she really enjoyed talking to them was when she was explaining something that mattered to her. She couldn't stand actually listening to them. Freyja worked quietly alongside them. They talked about boys and shoes. It was all boring until one of them said something that made Freyja pay attention.

"That Jay, he's pretty lame, eh?"

"Yeah, what's with always being so *busy*?"

"Do you think he was at another party?"

"Nah. I doubt that."

"If he was, it was probably some kind of dweeby role-playing thing."

The girls laughed.

"You mean Sanjay?" Freyja asked, just to be sure.

"Yeah. Jay."

"Oh. He introduced himself as Sanjay," Freyja said.

"We've been calling him Jay."

"I never noticed."

How was it possible that these girls did not think that Sanjay was as cute as Freyja thought he was? She couldn't ask, of course. It would reveal way too much. But the girls weren't done guessing about Sanjay.

"Even when he's here, he's rushing around."

"Yeah. What's up with that?"

"Maybe he's responsible?" Freyja suggested.

The girls looked at her like she'd barged in and was clueless about how unwelcome she was. They looked back at each other. It was like they were speaking a silent language. They dropped the subject completely and moved on to eyeliner.

Freyja tried to picture herself in Ottawa again. She would wreak havoc with placards and crowds. She would . . . But she couldn't get the image back. It was like she needed to be on the soapbox in order to believe that the soapbox was real.

In her mind's eye, she saw Angela Davis, Anita Sarkeesian, and Roxane Gay. She saw the steps at Parliament Hill. She saw Elizabeth May, Libby Davies, and Jenny Kwan. She wanted to see herself there among them.

But right now, she was up to her elbows in disgusting filth. She didn't have a soapbox. She didn't even look like someone who knew what soap was.

12 Two Against the World

FREYJA GATHERED HER STUFF from her locker at the food bank. She put on her coat and reminded herself that she needed to sign out. The door opened behind her. It was Sanjay, coming down from the upstairs office.

"You're still here?" He glanced at his phone and stuffed it back into his pocket.

"I'm slow," she said. She was wrenching her arm back, trying to find the armhole in her jacket.

Why did it seem like he always caught her in the middle of doing something embarrassing?

"Here," he said. He grabbed the edge of her jacket to make it easier.

"God, what am I? In Kindergarten?"

"Jackets are hard," he joked. "I get caught in mine all the time."

"You do not," Freyja said.

"Okay. I don't."

She shook her head at him. "Why are *you* still here? I thought you'd left?"

"I've got more to do. I'll be here for a while. Actually, I was going to take a break. I'll walk you out."

"Okay," Freyja said. "You can remind me to sign out then."

"Aren't you reminding yourself right now?"

She pursed her lips together and gave him a glance.

Outside, he asked if she was getting picked up or walking. Freyja explained she needed to go downtown to grab some pamphlets from the queer resource centre. She was going to catch the bus.

"I'll wait with you," Sanjay offered.

"You don't mind?"

He shook his head. It was raining. Sanjay took his hands out of the pockets of his hoodie and pulled the hood up over his head. Freyja opened her black umbrella.

"Want to share?" she asked.

"I'm all right," he said.

But as they started walking, he took the umbrella from her. "Let me."

"Okay."

Their arms brushed lightly as they neared the bus stop. Freyja could feel the warmth from his arm, but tried not to. She was sure it was nothing.

"For someone who dislikes humanity, you're pretty nice," Freyja observed.

"I don't dislike everyone." Sanjay glanced sideways at her without turning his head.

She did the same.

"How did you get to be so messed up?" Freyja asked. "What trauma did you go through?"

"Nothing, I don't think." Sanjay looked like he was trying to remember. "Anyway, it's pure logic."

"That the world is going to hell?"

"Yes."

"And we'll all have to fend for ourselves? Like wolves. Or like in *Lord of the Flies*."

"Yep. Totally logical." He smiled.

"You're twisted."

"What about you?"

"Abandonment issues. My mom left when I was little. Even now when I talk to her she's not interested."

"I'm sure she is."

"Maybe. But she's more interested in birds." Freyja took out her phone and showed Sanjay the pictures that her mom had sent to her from her research station up north. Freyja realized the barren landscapes reminded her of the chilly relationship she had with her mom.

Sanjay paid close attention. He asked a lot of questions. Before she knew it, Freyja had told him pretty much everything. How her dad and Gram tried to make up for her mom not being around.

How her mom didn't know who her daughter really was. And didn't seem to want to know.

"You know what's weird?" Freyja said. "I don't normally open up to people like this. And we've known each other, what, a couple of weeks? And you have my whole life story."

"Yeah, same here," Sanjay said.

"You're like my brother from another mother," Freyja said. She laughed at her own joke.

Sanjay didn't laugh. He looked at his feet.

"What are you doing later?" he asked.

"After I get home? I dunno. Dinner. Homework. I told myself I'd finally do that video blog, but . . ." she shrugged.

"Yeah, how's that going?"

"It isn't."

"How come?"

"It's different now. I feel like people started to want Rachel. I don't want to disappoint them."

"You won't."

"I don't even know what to talk about anymore."

"Just share what's new with you."

"Yeah, but I've been pretty boring since Rachel and I broke up."

"Is it because you miss Rachel?"

"Nah, I'm starting to feel over her."

"You are?"

"Yeah, I don't think I told you . . ."

"You haven't told me anything."

"Well, she's with someone new already. And . . . I don't know. I thought it'd hurt more. It hurts. But, like, there's also stuff I don't miss. Maybe we weren't really as connected as I thought. I hate to admit it, but I think maybe she's kind of shallow. And maybe I was more shallow when I was with her, or our relationship was. I don't really know. It's confusing."

Just then, the bus appeared in the distance.

"Quick," said Freyja. "Let's do this." She pointed her camera toward their faces to snap a selfie. "Let's do a screw-the-world picture."

Their faces looked back at them from the small, lit-up rectangle of Freyja's phone. They both put a middle finger up and scowled. When she looked at the image, it made Freyja laugh. The photo Freyja captured was of Sanjay looking ready to kill someone. She was glancing sideways at him, smiling. They looked at it together. She texted it to him and they both posted it online right away.

"I'm glad you feel like you can open up to me," Sanjay said.

"You really are like a brother or something."

Freyja didn't know why she needed to stress it again. It's not like she had siblings to compare this thing with Sanjay to. Maybe if he really was her brother, she might not feel the connection to him that she felt. But there was something different in the way they were together.

Without a word, Sanjay collapsed the umbrella neatly into its small shape and handed it to her. The folding door opened and Freyja stepped up, held her bus card to the scanner, and looked back around to say goodbye to Sanjay, but he had already turned to walk away.

As she packed herself into the back corner of the crammed bus, Freyja thought about Sanjay. What was it? He was kind to her, that was for sure. He had a way of looking out for her. She took her phone out of her pocket and looked at the picture again. She tried to see it as a stranger would. The snapshot captured a stolen glance. If someone looking at it didn't know Freyja was queer, they might think she had a crush on this guy.

But she didn't. She couldn't. No matter what she'd just said about Rachel, she was still dealing with breakup pain. This was emotional rebound. Freyja needed to feel safe from the danger of romantic feelings. Who could be safer than Sanjay?

The rain poured down the steamy windows. Freyja put on her headphones. Something heavy weighed on her. It was the face Sanjay made when she told him — twice — that he was like a brother. He looked heartbroken.

13 Questions

EVERY WEEK FOR OVER A YEAR, Freyja and Rachel had done a video blog. And now it had been ten weeks and nothing. Freyja scrolled through new comments: "Where r u?" and "Waaaz up?"

But what was there to say?

Sure, she could talk about the walkout she wanted to organize. But then she'd make the GSA sound bad. She'd sound all bitter about not being a glittery, sparkly *Glee*-cast type of person. She could talk about food justice. But it was different. And right now, it was something she wanted to keep for herself.

She was trying to figure out how to start when she noticed her mom's Skype status listed as "online." That was rare. Should she try calling her mom?

She figured it was worth a shot.

Freyja's mom was just out of the shower. Her hair was in a towel and she was wearing a robe.

"If it had been anyone but you, I wouldn't have answered," her mom said. She patted her head and rubbed the towel around.

"I just saw your online light come on," Freyja said, almost defensively.

"Yeah, we're back at the station tonight, picking up some supplies, sending some data. This was the first proper shower I've had in weeks."

"Whoa. So how's it going up there?"

"The north is beautiful, honey. I wish I could have you up here with me, but . . . "

"Too dangerous, I know. Have you seen any arctic ptarmigans yet?"

"Yeah, nine days ago. We got lucky. Sarah had a feeling. And sure enough, there was a whole flock. We managed to tag one."

"Wow."

"Yeah. We've been tracking them ever since. They're almost impossible to see in the tundra. They blend in so perfectly with their surroundings."

"Yeah." When Freyja was just a little girl, her mom had described white plumage against white snow to her.

"I took a photo of the northern lights for you, Freyja. But it's so hard to . . ."

". . . really get them in a photo. I know," Freyja interrupted. Her mom spent her whole life with things that were almost impossible to capture.

"How's your dad?" Freyja's mom asked.

"Oh, you know, the usual."

"Yeah, I figured. No news is good news with him."

Freyja thought about that. It wasn't really true. Her dad always had news. But he only shared things when he knew you had time for them and wanted to hear them. He wasn't going to call up his ex in the north to tell her about the totally rad tattoo he did the other day. It was the truth and it was a super-huge deal for him. He had gone on about it over dinner the other night. But Freyja didn't say anything. She decided her mom didn't deserve to know.

Freyja hadn't even told her mom about volunteering at the food bank. No news of her own ever seemed big enough next to her mom's adventures. So when her mom asked what was new with her, she answered, "Nothing much."

"How are you doing? Getting over Rachel?"

"Oh, that. It's going, I guess."

"You just have to pour yourself into something else, sweetie. All that passion of yours. It can't be contained. You'll find love again."

"Yeah. I know." Freyja knew she should show gusto. She should sound optimistic. She should show the fighting spirit everyone said she and her mom had in common. But she didn't feel like it.

"So is the GSA stuff going all right?" her mom asked.

"Yeah."

"School?"

Freyja shrugged. "Same as always."

"Well, don't forget you've got free tuition, so get those . . ."

"Grades up . . ." Freyja finished her mom's sentence. All they ever did was repeat old conversations.

She thought about Sanjay. He couldn't tell his parents about his plans, either. Sometimes it was just better to stay silent on the things that matter the most.

That night, Freyja couldn't sleep. She tossed and turned. At 1:30 in the morning, she heard her phone ding with a message. It was Sanjay.

"Still up?"

"Of course."

"Question. Do you want to come with me to India this summer?"

"Of course."

He sent her back a happy face. She waited for more, but that was it.

What a strange guy, she thought. *Strangely perfect.*

The GSA meeting had an official time and place. But apart from that, the core members would hang out at a table just outside the cafeteria. It was like a coffee shop that wasn't. It was a big table just like the ones inside. It had the same fluorescent lights above. But it was just a bit different from sitting in the cafeteria.

Freyja picked up some fries. No burger. No gravy. She thought of chickens and of world hunger. She didn't like ketchup much. She especially didn't like the way the pump was never clean. And how the ketchup came out like a disgusting turd that sat in the corner of the greasy paper rectangle.

"What are you doing for protein?" Katrina wanted to know.

"Glad you asked." Freyja was ready for the question. "I have this." She pulled a snack-sized pre-packed container of hummus out of her bag. It came with pretzels packaged on top.

"Okay, good," said Katrina. "I don't want you to faint or anything."

"I won't."

Kelsey, Claire, and Yolanda walked by and looked at Freyja. Usually they ate with Freyja. She waved, as she normally did, but they didn't wave back. They just stared.

"That was odd," Freyja said as the girls disappeared into the crowded cafeteria.

"Not really," said Katrina. "They think it's true."

"They think what's true?"

"Uh . . . that you're straight now?"

"Say what?"

"Well, are you? I was going to ask. But I thought it'd be rude."

"Katrina, you just did ask."

"Oh, yeah." Katrina smacked her forehead, playing dumb.

Freyja took out her phone. She'd looked at the photo she had taken with Sanjay well into the night. But she hadn't looked at it yet today. Now she did.

Beneath it, people had posted little hearts and cute emojis. She scrolled down the comments. They were from John and her friends from the GSA, and a lot of people she barely knew.

"Oh, shit," she said to Katrina. "So people think this means . . ."

"He's your boyfriend, isn't he? I mean, why else would you be looking at him like that?"

"No. I don't know. We're friends. We like each other. Like normal people like each other. Like I like you. If you and I posted a picture exactly like this, no one would make it weird. What the hell is wrong with people?"

Katrina shrugged.

"And why would they snub me for having a boyfriend?"

"So is he your boyfriend?" Katrina looked confused. "Or isn't he?"

Freyja didn't answer. Instead, she announced, "The GSA needs to have a serious discussion about policing each other. There are lots of letters in the

LGBTQ alphabet soup, for God's sake."

"Yeah, but . . ."

"But what?"

"Well, don't take this the wrong way or anything . . ."

"What?"

"You're kind of a loud *L* in that alphabet soup."

"What the hell is that supposed to mean?" Freyja snapped.

Katrina gestured with her hand. The look on her face said, "See what I mean?"

Freyja couldn't believe it. "I'm too loud now? Too outspoken? I guess it's fine when we need someone to do a speech or facilitate a meeting. Then it's always 'get Freyja.' But when I'm feeling something, I'm not allowed to express it. I'm supposed to be all quiet and ladylike."

Very gently, Katrina said, "I think people just want to know if you have a boyfriend."

Freyja snorted and crossed her arms.

"So that's a no?"

14 *Yes or No*

FREYJA STORMED OFF TO HER LOCKER. She grabbed her emergency cigarette and headed outside.

Since when were guys and girls not allowed to take photos together? Everyone did that. Everyone. There wasn't a single person around who wasn't in some kind of cute group photo with someone glancing at them. Thousands of social media uploads scrolled past her mind's eye. She was certain.

Why was she being singled out?

Out in the smoke pit, she couldn't light up fast enough. She inhaled and sat down, still reeling from the strange looks from the girls who were supposed to be her friends. She took out her phone to look at the picture again.

Damn, Sanjay was adorable in it. Freyja noted that the picture showed her looking at ease. Sanjay brought that out in her. He was easy to be around. She had just shared so much with him and it showed in her smile. The way she'd felt when she'd taken that photo was the complete opposite of what she was feeling now. She was stuck at school with judgy people who pretended to be allies. But all they really wanted was a sensational headline in the live-action version of TMZ that was high school. Ugh.

She had tagged Sanjay when she posted the picture. She pressed her thumb to his name and followed the link to where the photo appeared on his account. He'd received some comments too. Mostly thumbs up emojis, a few people saying "so cute!" and a laughing monkey. Because every photo gets a laughing monkey for reasons no one can explain. Sanjay's school was clearly not full of the same sort of aliens Freyja had to deal with.

She texted him: "People are insane."

Two seconds later, she saw the dots. He was writing an answer.

"That's why you have to learn to live off the land."

She looked at his text.

So logical.

The world is a mess.

People are idiots.

The answer is wilderness.

Hmmm.

"What about bears?"

"What? This?" He sent her a picture of an adorable panda bear cub.

Why did Sanjay have to be so damn cute?

She scrolled through her phone and took a long drag off her cigarette.

Oh shit. Her calendar snapped her back to reality. It was Thursday. She was sitting out here feeling sorry for herself, and the GSA was already fifteen minutes into their meeting. She dropped the butt of her cigarette onto the asphalt and squished it with her foot.

She ran inside and up the brightly painted stairwell of Hall C. She was nearly panting when she opened the door to the classroom where the meeting was being held.

There was John. He was at the front of the room, holding court. He didn't even look at Freyja when she entered.

"Sorry I'm late," she said.

"It's fine," he said. "I've got this."

He gestured for her to sit down. It was the same gesture Freyja had given John all those times he arrived late. How could she respond to a gesture like that? She found a chair and sat down.

"As I was saying," John continued. He sounded like a teacher who'd been rudely interrupted. "We have a small budget."

"A tiny budget," Freyja burst out. "As in no budget."

"We have a *small* budget." John made his voice louder and clearer, as if to drown her out. "And I was thinking we could stretch it. We could make sequined overhangs and a disco ball. Maybe we can borrow some strobe lights."

"Are you for real?" Freyja asked. "We have money for a poster. That's it. And anyway, what about the trans rights protest? I don't remember voting."

"I'm facilitating this meeting," John said. His icy tone told her to shut up. Or else.

"Whatever, then." Freyja rolled her eyes. In her mind, she defended the whole mess to the principal. She saw herself explaining how John had hijacked the meeting and made stupid choices.

"We could probably also get a smoke machine," Vanessa said. "My older sister checks coats at a club. She might be able to borrow theirs."

"No way! Amazing!" John said.

"And I know someone with a sewing machine," Vanessa added. "So we could do costumes."

"Where are you going to get the money for fabric?" Freyja asked. Had they all lost their minds?

"We'll fundraise," answered John.

"But the whole event *is* a fundraiser," Freyja objected.

Vanessa turned on Freyja. "Why are you being mean?"

Rachel looked at Vanessa, then at Freyja, then back at Vanessa. It was tense.

"I'm not being mean. I'm being realistic," Freyja said.

"All in favour of putting John in charge of the assembly number?" Vanessa asked the group, ignoring Freyja.

Hands shot up. John's and Vanessa's, obviously. And Rachel's. Katrina's didn't. But Katrina had just finished dissing Freyja in other ways.

"Fine," Freyja said. She was almost in tears. No one would know it except Rachel, but Rachel had made her choice.

Freyja had become an expert at muffling her feelings in public. She mused that the club could go bankrupt and no longer exist. And then the kids who really needed it wouldn't have any place to go.

Freyja left. There was no sense in staying any longer. These people just wanted to put on some five-minute performance for Diversity Day.

Math class was next. Snoozefest. Freyja sat at the back of the room, feeling stupider by the minute. Her life was in shambles. Again. That was the worst part. She'd been alone and ignored before. She had vowed never to return. But here she was.

Her phone buzzed. It was Rachel. "You know people are talking. I told everyone there's no way in hell you're dating a dude. So don't worry."

Don't *worry*? Freyja stared at her phone. She pictured Rachel's expression. She reviewed her thought process. Rachel was on her spare block, and Freyja imagined her telling Vanessa and probably other curious morons all about her. She would claim to be an expert on Freyja, offering an insider's perspective. That was one thing about Rachel that Freyja didn't miss. Rachel loved being in the know. She loved having information and sharing it. She got some kind of power trip from it.

Freyja wrote back: "Thanks. But you don't know me as well as you think."

She needed Rachel to understand that she had grown. Freyja wasn't the open book she had once been. At least, not open to Rachel. And, weirdly enough, she had met someone who understood her better than Rachel ever did. What that meant, Freyja really couldn't say.

Rachel replied, "So UR dating him?"

Freyja couldn't answer. It wasn't as simple as that. There was no yes or no answer. If she wrote "no," she would be lying. But if she wrote "it's complicated," she might as well write "yes." So the best answer was no answer.

She went over the events at the GSA meeting in her head. John was behind this whole thing. He'd been too nosy in French class about the texts from Sanjay. He'd always paid a little too much attention to what Freyja was doing.

Freyja realized she had an enemy.

15 Bully

FREYJA CAUGHT UP with him in the hallway after school.

"John!"

He turned. "Heee-eey!" He was dressed in khakis and a pastel sweater. He flashed a bright, dimply smile. It was as if he was in clothing ad. "John, can I talk to you?" Freyja's voice was stern.

He stopped in his tracks and waited for Freyja to get to where he was standing.

"Uh, I don't even really know what to say right now," said Freyja. "Except to tell you that a guy and a girl can be friends without it being something more than that."

"Who are you talking about?"

"Me and my *friend* Sanjay. I know you're saying we're a thing."

"I didn't say anything."

"Your row of hearts said it all," Freyja snapped. "And I'm pretty sure no one else would have cared if you hadn't told them to. I thought you and I were friends. I thought we were allies."

"Well, then why do you undermine me all the time?"

"What?" Freyja didn't have a clue what he was talking about. It was John who was trying to take away her power, not the other way around.

"Take today. I was running the meeting. And you waltzed in late and totally tried to take over."

"I was just pointing out that you messed up on the budget."

"No, you were trying to control everything. You were doing what you always do."

Freyja arched her eyebrows in disbelief.

John looked at Freyja like she'd just landed from the moon. "Honey, ever since you transferred here, you've needed to be in control. You've run that club like you're the only queer who's ever suffered. And the rest of us are sick of it."

"Oh, so now the whole GSA hates me."

"They don't hate you. But they are ready for a change."

If John is the change they want, Freyja thought, *they are welcome to it*. "Whatever," she said. "Going over the budget endangers the whole club. But I guess you can handle that. Do what you want."

Freyja turned and walked away.

She took the bus home, sitting at the back with her headphones on. She wanted to block out the whole world and all the stupid people in it.

She regretted posting the photo of herself with Sanjay. But she didn't regret what happened between them that afternoon. The real connection had meant so much to her. She remembered feeling like he understood her. She told him things she never told anyone. She didn't have friends she talked to, not like that. But she felt like Sanjay could handle anything she had to say. He could take it and hear it and live with it and not judge her. He had been supportive of her videos. And he admired her even though she was an out lesbian, or maybe because of it.

But lesbians don't have sex with guys — or date them, or make out with them, or anything. That was what the word meant. And that's what made Freyja trust Sanjay. He'd stand beside her with nothing to gain from it. No, no matter what it might cost her, she did not regret that afternoon. She decided she did not regret taking the photo. Or posting it and showing the world that there was someone in her life that she cared about.

Freyja was sitting in her room. She was trying to gather up the nerve to call Sanjay. She wanted to talk to him about the photo and everything that happened that day. Then her phone rang. It was Sanjay.

"Hey," he said. "So there's this medicine walk coming up. A Musqueam elder is going to take a bunch of people out to Pacific Spirit Park. He'll be teaching how to live off of local plants and herbs."

"Oh yeah," Freyja answered. "I saw the poster for that." It had been up at the food bank.

"I was wondering if maybe you're thinking of going. I'm thinking of going. If you were going, we could maybe go together. I mean, we could ask other people to go too. But it'd be cool if you wanted to."

Freyja wanted clarity. "Are you asking me out on a date?"

"No, no. There could be other people. A whole group." He paused. "Unless you think it's best if it's just the two of us. Seeing as we hate most people.

But no, it wouldn't have to be a date. Like, we don't have to have dinner or anything."

"So if there's no dinner, it's not a date?"

"I guess if it's a date, there's usually some kind of food."

Freyja noticed he was talking too quickly. He didn't sound like himself. Was he nervous? "So if we don't eat, it's not a date?"

"Oh my God. Do you want to go or don't you?"

"Yeah, I want to. Let's go."

After they got off the phone, Freyja squealed into her pillow. Was she a total monster or what? She just agreed to go on a date-like thing with a guy, knowing she was feeling complicated emotions about him and about her sexuality and identity and about all of it. She should have told him. She could have put on the brakes right here, right now. She knew she was sending him all the wrong signals. She hated herself for it.

Later that night, Rachel's smiling picnic face appeared on her phone's screen. The second she answered, Freyja vowed to herself not to talk about Sanjay. Not even once.

"So . . . this guy from the food bank," Rachel began.

Freyja completely ignored the prying. "Actually, I'm glad you called. I have to ask you about John."

"Oh yeah?"

"Yeah. Well, you saw how he took over today. And you know as well as I do that he's gossiping about me. Is he staging a coup or something?"

"John? No. He's just taking what he learned from you and going in his own direction."

"I did not teach him that some musical number is more important than human rights."

"Freyja, you have got to let the Beyoncé thing go. You're going to give yourself an ulcer."

"I just can't believe that the whole GSA is ready to throw trans students under the bus. And yet there you all are, having a field day about the whole boyfriend/ not boyfriend thing at my expense."

"You're impossible. You know that?" Rachel

snapped. "John is standing up to you because you've spent the last couple of years putting him in his place."

"What? Is that what he's saying?"

"Freyja, it's what we all know. It's what we've all seen. You can be a bit of a bully."

"What?" She couldn't believe what she was hearing. "*You* think I'm a bully? Everyone thinks I'm a bully?" The idea made Freyja want to cry. It made her wish that Rachel was there with her so she could rest her head on her chest and sob into her embrace.

"Well . . ." Rachel hesitated. "You're strong, and you like having things your way."

"But I'm always thinking about other people. What's best for the GSA, what's best for queer youth, all of that."

"But you have your own idea of what's best for everyone. You think that the group is all that matters. Maybe you need to just let people do their thing. I mean, groups are made up of people."

"Wow. I can't believe this." Freyja couldn't hold back the tears any longer. She knew that Rachel could

tell she was starting to cry. But it didn't matter. Rachel had seen it all before.

"I didn't mean to hurt your feelings," said Rachel. "I probably shouldn't have told you."

"No, no. I'm glad you did." Freyja sniffled and wiped her nose on her sleeve. "I should go."

"Are you okay?"

"Yeah."

Freyja sobbed into her pillow. She'd been so sure she was doing what was right for trans students, for the future of the school and the GSA. She never thought she might be coming on too strong or seem too controlling. But what Rachel had said made sense.

She wanted to call Sanjay, but she was afraid he'd make her feel better. And she didn't deserve to feel better. She didn't deserve an amazing conversation about world politics and the rise of organic farming. It was easy — too easy — to get sucked into Sanjay's world. A world where someone got her. Was that what she wanted? To live a life of what? Happiness? Love?

All her life, Freyja had taken things seriously. That was who she was. She was the girl who stood for something. But had she screwed up? Had her ego caused her to let down the very people she wanted to help? If so, she had to face that head on. She couldn't indulge in whatever it was she felt for Sanjay. Especially because she didn't even know what that was.

16 When Words Matter

FREYJA HOVERED IN THE FOYER of the food bank, waiting to sign in. When there was no sign of Sanjay, she dumped her soaked jacket and umbrella in the locker. She went out to the warehouse, where she saw the back of Sanjay's head as he directed a guy backing Dan's truck into the loading area. Her heart sank. Everything in her was in pain because she knew what she needed to do. And now she had to do it in the middle of the warehouse.

She walked up and tapped him on the shoulder. When he turned, his eyes lit up with a sparkle that she'd only seen when he was talking to her.

"Hey," he said. He cracked a goofy smile.

"We have to talk," she said.

"Uh oh. That doesn't sound good."

"It isn't."

"Okay, give me just a second." He went to the driver's side of the truck and said something that Freyja could not hear. She reminded herself it was now or never. She could only hold her tears back for so long.

He walked toward the office space and she followed. They walked past the Wall of Shame with all the old food items. She saw the ranch dressing pouch she found on the day she first met him.

In the office, Dan was hunched over a binder. He looked up and did a double take. Sanjay must have had a look on his face because Dan got up right away. He announced he was going to go make himself some coffee. He closed the door on his way out.

Sanjay gestured toward the desk chair. "Here. Sit."

Freyja did. He took the smaller metal chair next to it.

"What's up?" he asked.

She started sweating, she was so nervous. Sanjay turned on the small fan that was on the desk and pointed it at her.

"Better?" he asked.

"Yeah," she said.

"Okay. Continue."

"It's about that photo. Of us."

"Yeah?" His eyes lit up again.

"Did you see all the weird comments under mine?"

"What comments?"

He whipped out his phone. He looked angry, like he was ready to defend her, to rescue her. He scrolled through the stuff she'd agonized over. Then his smile came back. "You mean all the hearts and shit?"

She nodded. "People at my school are kind of messed up. They think . . . I don't know why they're so stupid. But they think we're, like, a thing."

"Okay." He leaned toward her.

"And we're not."

"Okay . . ." He sat back.

He looked like he was waiting for her to say more. She felt like she'd said everything that needed saying. She was surprised he didn't get it. "I mean, we can't be. So . . . it's a problem," she said.

"Okay."

"Can you say anything else right now? Please?"

"Um . . . I don't know what you want me to say."

"Well, what do you think? Did anyone say anything to you?"

"Nah, not really. My friends think you're cute is all." He looked down at the floor.

"But then you told them that I'm your friend or whatever. I mean, I guess that's the thing. The 'whatever' is a problem. I don't know what we are."

He looked into her eyes. "What do you want us to be?"

"I'm queer."

He shrugged. "You're you."

"What's that supposed to mean?"

He shook his head, like he regretted his words. He looked like her dad always did when Freyja started an argument with him. "I'm not sure."

"I can't be with you. I can't have a boyfriend. Even that word. Boyfriend. It's not right for me. There's no room in my life for that word."

"You don't have to use that word, you know. You could call me anything you want."

"But . . . okay. What do you want? Let's say you know nothing at all about me. I'm just some random girl."

"Well, you're not a random girl. And I do know stuff about you."

"But just pretend for a sec."

"I don't need to. What I know about you, that's what I like. There. That's my final answer. It doesn't matter to me if you think of yourself as a lesbian."

She cut him off, saying, "I *am* a lesbian."

"Whatever. The labels don't matter. I just like you. I like spending time with you."

"As friends."

"As whatever."

"This is so confusing." She repeated the word, making each syllable separate, "Con. Few. Zing."

"It doesn't have to be. Don't get all stressed out about it." He took her hands in his and held them. It was the sort of thing that would look romantic if someone saw it from far away. Up close, it made Freyja nervous.

She liked him too. She didn't want to break his heart or be mean or lead him on. But she didn't want to abandon queer causes or be straight. She wanted none of those things. What she couldn't tell was what she did want. She pulled her hands from his grasp. "I can't do this."

Freyja couldn't look at Sanjay. She walked out of the office, went to her locker, grabbed her coat and umbrella. She ran out. She didn't sign out. She didn't look back to see if Sanjay was coming after her. She just hurried into the rain and let it hit her. *Let the rain drench me*, she thought. She was cold. Her teeth were chattering by the time she was at Commercial Drive.

But it didn't matter. She held her coat like a package, clutching it to her chest. She cried as she walked. It was okay because it was raining out. Without having her umbrella up, with rain falling from her face, no one would be able to tell.

Freyja saw how ugly the world was. There was a hand-drumming hippie sitting in McSpadden Park. He had trinkets spread out in front of him. She'd seen him a million times and always admired his way of being. He was just doing his own thing, resisting mainstream culture. But today, something about him bothered Freyja. He looked at her. Why was he looking? She walked by him, ignoring his stare.

"Hey," he said to her. "You should really smile more."

She gave him the finger.

17 Working It Out

FREYJA LAY DOWN ON HER BED. She was exhausted from having too many feelings. Still fully clothed, she pulled the covers over herself. She curled into a ball with her knees tucked in front of her. Maybe if she covered herself, she could disappear. And if she disappeared, her feelings would go away too.

This was not the behaviour of a fighter. She was not the champion she wanted to be. This was total and complete failure.

Her phone vibrated. It was a text from Sanjay.

"I don't get you."

What could she say to that? What was there to say? She texted back: "I suck. I'm sorry."

She hit *Send. That's it, I guess,* she thought. The end. She could get out of going to the food bank. She'd never have to see him again. And the whole mess would just go away.

That's when Freyja really started crying. This wasn't just tears rolling down her face. She sobbed until her insides ached. Then she cried some more.

Days passed. Freyja slinked around the school, hoping she wouldn't get noticed. She emailed the food bank's address — not Sanjay's — and she said she had to focus on schoolwork.

Gram sat with her night after night. Freyja had nothing to say, so Gram did Sudoku. Gram never asked Freyja to tell her about it. On the third night, Freyja spilled it.

"It kills me that I've become this person," Freyja said. "I used to not give a crap what anyone thought. Now I've let what people think hold me back from . . ." She turned over, planted her face in her pillow, and moaned.

"It's okay if you like him." Gram cut right into the core of it. "Even if you love him."

"Who said anything about love?" Freyja started to cry.

Gram put her hand on Freyja's shoulder. "It's confusing. I know."

"I'm not confused," said Freyja. "By the way, it's what people always say to bisexuals. That they're confused."

"Hmph." Gram tapped her pen on the newspaper and rolled her eyes.

"What?" Freyja asked meekly.

"You've never used that word before. *Bisexual*, not *confused.*"

"I don't know what other word I can use. I loved Rachel, you know. And so I don't understand this. I'm more choked up over this thing with Sanjay then I was when Rachel dumped me. It's like he's taken over my mind. He's all I think about. And that's really scary. I used to have all these causes."

"Is that what this is about? Causes?" Gram laughed. "Only you could make this about activism."

"Activism is all I've got."

"Who says you have to give that up? I mean, he's got causes."

"Yeah, but I don't want to get sucked into his stuff. I don't want to wake up one day and realize I've been fighting the wrong fight."

"What if you two are fighting the same fight?"

"But he's into food access — clean water, seed banks. And I'm into queer issues."

"So?" Gram said firmly. "You're both fighting for human dignity."

"I guess." Freyja was quiet for a while. Gram went back to solving Sudoku until Freyja let out a long sigh. "It's so different, how I feel. With Rachel, in the beginning, I was so sure about it. I was so completely into it."

Gram leaned forward. "Love feels different every time."

"Really? Because what I feel about Sanjay is totally different. I'm obsessed. But I'm also afraid."

"Love is scary."

"It's terrifying. What if he doesn't like me as much as I like him? What if he goes away for real? He's got plans to move in the summer, you know. Not just to another town. To another continent halfway around the world. At first I didn't think he was serious. But what if he is? What if he really does want me to go with him? Even worse, what if he leaves me behind? I mean, I don't think I can handle having a boyfriend. It seems like such a strange thing for me to have. What do all those years of GSA stuff matter if in the end my soulmate is actually a guy?"

"So that's really what you're most afraid of?" Gram asked.

"No. I'm most afraid that I messed it up. I broke it off with Sanjay before anything could even start. And the scariest thing now is that I might never see him again. I'll be haunted forever by the thoughts of what could have been."

"You'll figure it out. You always do." Gram clasped Freyja's arm for a moment. Then she left.

Freyja was alone with the idea that maybe she and Sanjay hadn't been as doomed as she thought . . . but that she just doomed them. She had never asked him about India in person. Now it was too late. She couldn't just call or text him out of the blue and ask if he had meant that she should come. Or could she? She clutched her pillow.

Freyja called Sanjay. No answer. She waited fifteen minutes and called again. Nothing. Was he screening her? She figured it'd be fair if he was. But something in her told her that there was more to it than that.

She texted him the obvious. "Where R U?"

No answer. Nothing.

It was Friday night. He was likely at the food bank. She got dressed and put on her shoes. When Gram asked where she was going, Freyja said, "I need to see Sanjay."

Freyja rushed to the food bank. She'd gone days without talking to Sanjay. Now it felt like if she couldn't see him right away, she'd die. But he was nowhere to be found. Reception hadn't seen him. None of the volunteers had seen him. She knocked on the door to Dan's office. He opened it.

"I need to see Sanjay," Freyja said. She could tell she sounded panicked. "He isn't responding to my texts or calls."

"He's gone off the grid for a while. Camping."

"Are you kidding? It's December."

"He wanted to test out his new thermal sleeping bag."

"Do you know where he's gone? I really need to see him."

"I thought you ended it with him." Dan spoke carefully, as if he didn't know if he should trust Freyja.

"I messed up. I really, really messed up." Tears began to flow down her cheeks. Freyja thought about Sanjay outside in the cold. It was a clear night. And freezing. "And now he's going to freeze to death because of it."

Dan eyed her. "I'm under pretty clear instruction not to tell anyone where Sanjay has gone."

"Especially me, right?"

"You should have seen him these past few days. I don't know what went down between you two, and I don't need to. But, man, I've never seen him like that. And I've known him since he was a little kid."

"I have to see him. I have to make it right."

Dan let out a sigh. He tapped his fingers on the desk. "I probably shouldn't do this. I really shouldn't. My wife's gonna kill me." Dan reached into his back pocket and pulled out a ring of keys. He fumbled with them, then held them out to Freyja. "Take the Beast."

"For real?"

Dan went to the computer and pulled up an aerial view of North Vancouver. He showed Freyja the spot he had shown to Sanjay long ago. The perfect place to go where no one would bother him. Dan explained that you could get there by transit. But it was a truly unlikely place to camp. Therefore, it was an unlikely place to get caught camping.

"You're the only one who can work this out," he said to Freyja. "So do it. Go fix it."

"I will."

18 What It Is

FREYJA BUCKLED UP. She adjusted the seat and mirror. Never in her life had she driven anything like the Beast. She was used to taking an occasional Car2Go and felt okay driving a compact two-seater. The truck really was a beast. As she drove, she thought that everyone she knew would tell her that Sanjay's taking off was not her fault. But in her heart she knew that she had slammed the relationship door in his face. That was why he was outside in the freezing cold trying to make a point.

But Freyja could make a point as well as he could.

She drove across the Second Narrows Bridge and turned right onto the Dollarton Highway. The night was dark. She had the eerie sense that she was utterly alone on that stretch of highway.

She pulled into Cates Park and zigzagged her way through the layers of parking lots. She got out of the truck. Clutching her phone, the only light source she could think of, she walked toward the water. The sound of sticks cracked beneath her feet.

There it was. She saw a dome tent lit with a faint glow, sheltered by a patch of large evergreens.

It was past ten. The wind was rough on her face. She walked toward the yellowish dome, her heart beating fast. What could she say? Would he even talk to her?

Freyja called Sanjay's name, but nothing happened. It occurred to her it was possible that the tent contained some other lunatic. But she knew that wasn't true. It was Sanjay. It had to be him. She called his name again.

She got closer and closer to the tent, crushing tiny twigs in her path. Her steps seemed loud, even over the shrieks of wind. The tent was made of light fabric. But she couldn't just open it up and walk in. She found a tent pole and knocked. Tapped, really.

"Sanjay?"

She heard the zipper of the entrance opening. She heard his voice saying, "What the hell?"

Sanjay poked his head out and looked at her. She couldn't tell from the look on his face whether he was happy or angry to see her. But for sure he was surprised.

"What are you doing here?" he asked.

"I came to find you."

"Why?" He grimaced.

"I was worried."

"You don't have to worry about me. I'm not your thing to worry about."

"Sanjay . . ."

"Worry about ending homophobia and feeding the world. Don't worry about me. I don't need you to do that, okay?"

"I know you're mad."

"I'm not mad."

"Fine. Frustrated."

"I'm not frustrated."

"Fine. Whatever." She wrapped her scarf tighter as the wind howled. She should have worn more than her hoodie but there had been no time to think. Her nose was running from the cold.

"You're freezing," observed Sanjay. "Get in here."

"But you don't want to see me."

"I also don't want you to stand there shivering in front of me. I can't stand that. You know I can't."

He unzipped the tent entrance all the way. Freyja crouched down and ducked her head. She slipped her boots off and before she knew it, she was kneeling on his sleeping bag inside.

It was cozy, in a way. It was slightly warmer in the tent than outside. But Freyja still thought it was crazy to be out here in the middle of winter. There was a small lamp hanging from the very top. There was that mildew scent that seemed to come with all camping equipment, free of charge.

Sanjay took the blanket from on top of his sleeping bag and covered Freyja with it. She needed to blow her nose really badly. He noticed and searched for a tissue. When he passed one to her, she used it and honked out the most embarrassing sound. She stopped shivering.

"Sanjay . . ."

He turned away from her. She wanted him to look at her. But he wouldn't. *There is nothing worse than this,* she thought. It was quiet. The wind outside was the only sound. Sanjay's eyes were fixed on the ground. Freyja was cold. She knew she'd hurt him. She knew she could not repair it or take it back.

"I don't get you," Sanjay finally said. "I thought we had a real connection. But you shut it down. Why?"

She shrugged. It was the question she'd been trying to ask herself for days. Leave it to Sanjay to figure out a clear and simple way to ask it. "I don't know," she replied. It was the truth.

"If it's that you're still in love with Rachel, I get that. I can at least sort of wrap my mind around it."

"I'm not still in love with Rachel, though."

"Then it's that you won't give us a chance just because I'm a guy. I need you to know I find that really, really messed up. Because I feel like there's something between us."

"There is."

"I'm not your 'brother.'" He put air quotes around the word. She remembered that she had said it twice. She nodded. He was *not* her brother. "And we're not just friends."

"I know." She nodded again.

"Like, we're sooo not friends."

"Yeah," Freyja said.

"Because with friends, I don't want to do this." He touched her cheek.

The stroke of his thumb sent shivers all the way down Freyja's body. This was what she longed for, to be touched by him. For him to look at her the way he was doing right now. She sucked in her lips. He moved his thumb to her mouth and rested it on her clenched lips until she released them. Then he lifted his thumb and touched her lips again with the gentleness of a kiss. They stared at each other. Nothing had ever been so slow as his thumb on her bottom lip, running back and forth.

"I want to kiss you," he said.

"I want that too," she whispered.

"But if I kiss you, I will never want to stop kissing you. So I kind of need to know if you're just going to give up on me or what."

Freyja knew that no matter what her path was, no matter what she called herself or what others called her, she would not regret this moment. This was what she wanted.

She kissed him.

19 Top of the World

SANJAY TOOK FREYJA'S COLD FACE in his warm palms. He drew her closer. They kissed so long Freyja's lips began to hurt.

He pulled back.

"Why are you stopping?" she asked.

"To look at you. I want to look at you."

"No. Don't stop."

She kissed him again. He wrapped his arms around her. She was drowning in his scent, which reminded her of cedar. Freyja was cold from sitting on the ground. But she didn't notice until Sanjay's hands travelled downward, then up beneath her hoodie.

He pulled back once again, but not far. "You're freezing."

"I don't care."

"I care," he insisted. He wrapped a blanket around her.

"Just kiss me."

"Let's get out of here."

She didn't want to move. She was afraid moving would break the moment into a million pieces. She needed to hang on to it, this best first kiss of her life. She had been so unsure. But now she was sure. So sure.

But he was starting to roll up his sleeping bag.

"I'll help you pack this up," Freyja said.

"The tent?"

"Well, you're not still planning on sleeping out here, are you?"

He looked at her. "You'll give me a lift home?"

She nodded.

"Oh, thank God."

She laughed. Together they rolled up his sleeping bag, folded the other blankets, crammed everything into his backpack. As the tent came down, Freyja knew she had to say the stuff that had been on her mind.

"The idea of being with you scares me," Freyja said.

"Why? Because of my manliness?" He smiled his crooked smile.

"Because what if one day I leave you for a girl? Would that hurt you more than if a straight girl left you for a guy?"

The words sounded stupid as soon as she said them. Sanjay stopped what he was doing. He put the tent poles down on the ground and went to her. He took her hands in his and said, "Freyja, I don't want you to leave me at all."

"I'm just adjusting to this whole bisexual pansexual whatever thing."

"Stop being in your head so much. All that really matters is what's in your heart."

Freyja had never felt so much like herself before. Sanjay put his arms around her. She expected him to say more. But she realized as he held her that he was speaking without words. He looked deep into her eyes. She kissed him.

They got everything packed up. Freyja's nose started running again. Sanjay passed her another tissue and she blew into it. She hated the sound she made in the quiet night.

As they walked, Sanjay asked, "How did you find me, anyway?"

"Dan. I made him tell me."

"You're good," he said.

As they got to the parking lot, Sanjay was even more surprised. "Is that Dan's truck?"

"Yeah."

"You drove the Beast?"

She nodded.

"Holy shit." He looked impressed.

The truck doors creaked in the cold winter silence.

"Do you want me to drive from here?" he asked.

"Heck yeah," she said. She really had no idea how she'd managed to get the Beast there in the first place.

Once they were at Dollarton, Sanjay said he didn't want to go back home yet.

"What do you want to do instead?" Freyja asked.

"Well, we could go somewhere. Maybe somewhere kind of high."

"Like?"

He didn't say anything, but kept driving. Freyja read signs that showed they were nearing Mount Seymour. She got out her phone and texted Gram. "Found Sanjay. All good. Staying out a bit longer."

Gram texted back a "thumbs up" emoji.

Freyja felt safe with Sanjay at the wheel. They drove up higher and higher into the darkness. She was used to looking across the city, across the water, at the mountain they were driving up. Actually being there was a different thing. She looked out past snow piled along the highway to the city lights below. It made her feel like she was made out of light. At a lookout point, Sanjay pulled the Beast into a sharp U-turn and parked it so that they were facing the city. Though the city was not fully visible, its lights cast a glow that felt magical to Freyja.

"What now?" Freyja asked.

Sanjay turned off the engine. "More of this," he said. Sanjay gently put his palm behind her neck and pulled her close to him. They had their legs facing forward, but their bodies twisted to face each other. They kissed until their lips were chapped.

"I have an idea," Sanjay said. He scooted over the bench seat to be closer to Freyja. He gestured. "Come here."

"What? Sit on you?"

He nodded.

Freyja looked around. The windows were fogging up. Soon no one would be able to see in anyway. Nervous, she did as he said. Her right knee hit the armrest on the door. It hurt, but it didn't matter.

She straddled Sanjay, facing him. He put his hands up the back of her shirt, touching the skin of her back. The bulge in his pants was an unspoken mystery between them. She rubbed against it, wondering what it would be like to touch him there. She wanted to, but she couldn't. Not yet.

His travelling hands found the clasp of her bra and he undid it. She cursed the underwire. The fabric felt horrible, dangling loosely against her front. She wished it would just disappear. She squirmed.

"Is this okay?" he asked.

"Yes," she whispered.

His fingers inched around her sides. Skin that was always covered was now totally exposed, like her feelings. It made her shiver and sweat. But it was the biggest relief. He didn't touch her breasts. His fingers caressed the skin beneath them and beside them. It was as if he wanted to wait and not touch her at all. Finally, she couldn't take the teasing any more.

"You can touch me," she said.

He gulped. His eyes widened.

"Have you ever . . . like . . . before?" she asked when he didn't say anything.

He shook his head.

She lifted her shirt just enough to let her hands find his. She cursed the wire bra once more.

"Hold on," she said. One side of the wire stabbed into her like a knife. She moved his hands from her body and he let them fall. She used her best moves from gym class to remove her bra underneath her shirt. She pulled it out from her sleeve.

"Wow," Sanjay said. "That's impressive."

She laughed. "I'm like Harry Houdini."

The bra was on the drivers' seat now. Soon it would be too cold to wear. She took his hands in hers and kissed him on his palms. She guided them back beneath her sweater. She put them exactly where she wanted them to be and stared into his eyes. He looked scared but also confident. They didn't need words. They didn't even need to kiss. They stayed like that, transfixed. He touched her in his gentle way, holding her as if to show her just how precious she was to him.

"I don't want you to leave me for a girl," he said, his palms still cupping her. "But I would totally understand if you leave me for a girl. This is amazing."

She laughed. "You're amazing."

"Am I?"

She nodded.

He put his arms around her beneath her sweater. Warm, they caressed the skin of her back as he pulled her down to him. She rested on his chest and heard his heart beating.

"I want to hold you forever," he said.

She almost cried. The only thing in the world she knew for sure was that he meant it.

20 Both, and More

FREYJA HEARD SANJAY'S stomach growl. She was hungry too. "Want to get something to eat?" she asked.

"Are you asking me on a date?" he teased.

She laughed and pulled on her hoodie. He slid over to the driver's side. It was three in the morning. She was cold and her lips hurt.

"I'm not exactly presentable," she said.

"Grocery store?" He caressed the back of Freyja's hand. She felt somehow grown up, sitting next to him with her hand on his lap.

It was like Sanjay wanted to skip dating and go straight to domestic life. And Freyja loved it. He turned the ignition and they burned down the mountain highway to the twenty-four-hour grocer. The Safeway in the strip mall was closed.

Walking into the store with him, her hair all messy from his hands, she felt transparent. She felt like anyone who looked at them would know what they were up to. But she was strangely proud. She hadn't even bothered to put her bra back on. There was something satisfying about letting the truth hang out.

They walked together at first, very slowly. Sanjay held the basket and she held onto his arm. But soon, she had to go to the bathroom. She told him she'd return in a few minutes.

When she found him again, he was holding a frozen dinner. His face was serious. She thought for a second that he looked like an old man. A grumpy one. She laughed at the thought of it. She secretly hoped she would still be with him when they were old.

"American corporate greed is insane. There isn't a single real ingredient in this thing," Sanjay said. The rants were clearly not limited to the food bank.

Freyja laughed. "You can never turn it off, can you?"

In that moment, she thought of Rachel. Rachel always laughed at Freyja when she was serious. She had laughed even more at how Freyja had always taken it personally, was far too sensitive. And now Freyja was doing the same thing.

Sanjay said, "They're making billions off of people's ignorance. That's just wrong."

"I know," Freyja said. She smiled as she looked at him. Rachel had found Freyja's passion, her need to change the world, funny. Freyja was finding the same thing in Sanjay lovable. In her belly she knew she had fallen for him, that it was only a matter of time before she told him so.

She reached into the freezer and pulled out a marble cake. "What about this? It's Canadian, after all. And it's delicious."

"I've never tried one."

She jumped back. "You've *never* had marble cake? We're sooo getting it, then."

He grabbed it from her. He held it like he was continuing his lecture and it was a prop in his presentation. He studied the ingredient list and explained, "This is everything that's wrong with the world."

"Nope," Freyja said. "I disagree. This cake is not only tasty, it's the perfect symbol."

He furrowed his eyebrows.

Freyja took on the air of a teacher with the flair of a game show model showing off a product. Waving her hand over the rectangle that he held, she declared, "This cake is my sexuality."

"Don't tell me. I'm the chocolate."

"No because that would make Rachel the white cake. And she was so not vanilla."

He looked at her like he wasn't quite sure how to respond.

"As I was saying, these two flavours. It's not either/or. It's both . . . and more." She chuckled at herself. "That rhymes."

He rolled his eyes. He shook his head at her silliness. Then he grabbed her by the strings of her hoodie and pulled her close. In the middle of the freezer aisle, beneath the bright lights, they kissed once more.

"We're totally getting this," Freyja said again. She snatched the cake from his grasp and jogged to the checkout stand.

"All night?" Gram repeated. "It took you *all night* to convince him to pack up the tent?" The clock on the microwave showed it was 7:14 in the morning. Gram looked like she hadn't slept.

"Well . . . we went for a drive after," Freyja explained.

"Mmm hmmm," Gram said with a note of sarcasm. "I know what that means. I was young once too, you know."

They looked at each other. What had gone down

was obvious. Freyja was relieved she wasn't going to have to give details.

"I'm really tired. I'm going to get some sleep," she said, rising from a kitchen chair.

"Yes," Gram said. "You rest. And when you wake up, we'll have a good, long girl-to-girl conversation about condoms."

Freyja sighed. "Graaa-aam. It's not like that."

"Not yet."

"Okay, fine."

Though she would never admit it, Freyja was curious about what Gram would say. She'd done some research online. But she knew she wanted to hear it from the woman who'd lived through the sixties and seventies.

An hour later, Freyja's phone buzzed. It was Sanjay. "When can I see you again?"

"Aren't you tired? I thought we agreed to nap."

"All I can think about is seeing you."

They arranged to meet on the Drive. From far away, she saw him. He stood out among all the people on the sidewalk. He smiled at her when she was still a block away. It felt as though everyone else disappeared. When they got close to each other, he put his hands out and clasped hers. He pulled her in for a hug and a kiss.

They walked hand in hand.

"What do you feel like?" he asked.

"Coffee?" she said. She didn't care. All she wanted was to be near him.

"Sounds good."

As they walked together, she noticed something strange. The absence of looks. No one saw them. No one looked at them at all. That was unusual. Freyja and Rachel got looked at all the time. Often people smiled. Sometimes they didn't. Several times they were sneered at and once they were chased. Either way, people always noticed two girls hand in hand. But no one noticed her and Sanjay. Freyja thought about noting this to Sanjay. But then the need to talk about it passed. It was enough that his warm hand held hers and that he glanced sideways at her and smiled.

They got coffee to go and wandered over to the Cottonwood Community Garden. Freyja asked Sanjay about growing crops. He explained various tools and techniques used. He made it all seem simple.

"One day," he said, "People will tear up their lawns and grow food. It's already starting. And it'll happen more and more. In the future, there will be rooftop gardens on every building."

"Hold on. Are you saying there won't be a meltdown collapse and a world war over water?" she teased him.

"There might be. We'll have to wait and see."

"To see if people use their power for good or evil." She raised one eyebrow and rubbed her hands together like a villain.

He laughed. "Either way, you'll survive."

"You think?"

"You drove the Beast. You found me in the park. You can survive anything." He put his hand on her back as they walked in sync. "I asked before. Please say yes again. Come with me to Kolkata this summer."

She looked into his eyes that held so much promise. "When do we leave?"

"June. As soon as we graduate."

"Okay."

They kissed once more. For the first time in Freyja's life, everything was certain. She knew nothing about India or where they were going. She had no idea what they'd do when they got back to Canada. She didn't know if the world would end horribly or if Vancouver would turn into a hippie utopia with rooftop gardens and organic compost everywhere. But she knew that no matter what, she wanted to live it with Sanjay.

Freyja held her head high. She had nothing to hide, and no need to explain. She had found love, or something that could turn into love. And she would hold on to it, because that's what you do with love.

Freyja took her spot at the front of the room, ready to start the GSA meeting. John slouched in his seat. Freyja could tell he resented her being there. He was eager to take her place. And she'd let him . . . just as soon as she graduated and left the GSA behind.

"John," she started. "I just want to say that I know I've been bristly this year. If I've hurt you, I'm sorry. Sometimes I get really wrapped up in what I think we can get done as a group. And it's easy for me to forget that groups are made up of individuals."

John sat up.

"So let's spend the first fifteen minutes brainstorming how we're going to stage the walkout for Transgender Day of Remembrance. After that, John can lead a discussion on the musical number. We're a diverse bunch. We can do it all."

EPILOGUE

Freyja

SANJAY LIFTED FREYJA'S heavy suitcase onto the conveyor belt. Freyja took a deep breath. The past six months had been a frenzy of excitement. And it was only the beginning.

Her dad and Gram were holding it together, talking about what they'd have for dinner later. Fish sticks. And what they'd watch. Food Network.

Freyja pulled her cell phone from her back pocket and hit record.

"Well, beautiful faces, this is it. Out of the Closet is heading out of the country. The bags are checked. Next stop, Kolkata. I can't wait to share this summer with you guys. With me, you'll meet tons of interesting people and find out what matters to them. The list today is Why Who You Are Is Where You're Going . . ."

She posted her clip and stuck her phone back in her pocket. Sanjay put his arms around her and kissed her forehead. He checked their tickets as they walked toward the security gate.

"Ready?" she asked Sanjay.

"Whenever you are," he said.

"Okay. Let's go."

Acknowledgements

I'd like to thank Kat Mototsune for her guidance in this project, for seeing the characters clearly from the start and for being so generous in her edits.

I'm indebted to a community of writers who remind me that I am not alone even when I need to spend days by myself. They are: Tony Correia, Andrea Warner, Cathleen With, Jackie Wong, Billeh Nickerson, Shana Myara, Monica Meneghetti, and Karen X. Tulchinsky. I owe my sanity, stability, and self-esteem to the queer communities that have nurtured my complicated identities. As Freyja learns in this story, sexuality is fluid. It is extraordinary what happens when we allow ourselves and one another to see and be seen.

Thank you also goes to Elaine Yong and Cecilia Leong. So much of what I write is a product of our strange youth and their willingness to look out for me.

Much of this book was informed by my job at Directions Youth Services Centre where I'm part of running a meal program for homeless and at-risk youth. At work, I witness the alarming reality of food waste in Vancouver on daily basis and I'm keenly aware that without the help of the food bank and an amazing crew of volunteers, we could not provide these meals to the people who need them the most. Everyone deserves fair access to healthy food and I'm grateful to the many volunteers across Canada who, like Sanjay and Freyja, work to make the fundamental right to food easier for someone else. I'd like to give a shout out to the most wonderful coworkers anyone could hope for.

Thank you also to my mom, who taught me so much of what I know about food and cooking and life.

As always, thank you to Bren Robbins for listening to me talk about my characters as if they were real people, and for knowing when to take me away from my computer.